Every~ ~~
the ne~ ~~
the Tig~ ~~~~~~ ~~nal signal.

"Hut!"
Snap!

The ball almost stung, it came back so fast, but Buck didn't drop it. There was an explosion of pads and grunting bodies all around him. Buck jumped back two steps, forgetting about Marshall who was crossing the line on the right and looking instead to his left, where Chip should be charging around. Where the heck was he? Where—

Ooomph! A defensive body slammed into his left side, and the impact drove the air out of his chest, and felt like it was snapping ribs, but Buck instinctively held on tight to the football as he started to fall. He didn't make it down before another body crashed into him, but there was no more air to drive out, and Buck just crunched into the ground. He could smell wet earth inches from his face, and it smelled good, easy, comfortable. He could relax there.

Other books in the **BLITZ** series:

TOUGH TACKLE

Paul Nichols

BALLANTINE BOOKS ● NEW YORK

To Robert Hawks

RLI: $\dfrac{\text{VL: 6 \& up}}{\text{IL: 6 \& up}}$

Produced by the Jeffrey Weiss Group, Inc.
133 Fifth Avenue
New York, New York 10003

Library of Congress Catalog Card Number: 88-92155

ISBN 345-35109-6

Manufactured in the United States of America

First Edition: January 1989

THE TUCKER TIGERS

PLAYER	POSITION	YEAR	NUMBER
Brooks, Elwyn	DE	Jr	79
Bucek, John	WR-S	Sr	12
Burroughs, Ray	C-DT	Jr	98
Critchfield, Roger	HB	Jr	24
Danfield, Marshall	K-WR	Jr	00
Grover, Jim	OT-DT	Jr	72
Jackson, Norm	LB	So	45
Kildare, Matt	WR	Sr	15
LaRico, Tony	LB	So	51
Moorehead, Chip	FB	Sr	33
Mulbrauer, Carl	QB	Sr	6
Palmer, Brad	G	Sr	81
Porter, Jeff	LB-OT	Sr	57
Reiser, Pete	TE	Jr	18
Stapleton, Marc	Line	Sr	53
Tibbs, Billy	QB	So	10
Wainwright, Steve	HB-CB	Sr	20
Young, Buck	DE-OT	Jr	66

Head Coach: Doc Samuels
Assistant Coach: John Dunheim

ONE

Buck was charging in hard at defensive end, four feet behind the runner when the rain started, but he still managed to tackle the guy before getting spattered by a single drop of water. Launching himself off one foot, Buck hooked the runner's right arm, and both of them tripped forward in a cluster of tangled legs and cleats. Another halfback, Hank Chandler, scrambled to get out of the way of this avalanche, but didn't make it and got caught up in the tripping mess as well.

Chandler and the runner pinned behind him hardly had time for a quick yelp before they hit the ground hard. Two more defense men leaped on top of them as the whistle blew, and the guy at the bottom of the pile—

second-string receiver Marshall Danfield—
groaned and other voices in the pile joined
in.

"Take it easy, Buck, you almost broke my
neck."

"I think I lost a big tooth. No, wait. It was
my mouth protector."

"Are you clowns going to get off my leg,
or what?"

"Would somebody please move?"

"Watch it!" The rain was really coming
down now, and Buck pushed a wet arm out
of his face as he crawled up out of the pile.

"Excuse me for living," said Hank Chandler, the owner of the arm. "I'm just trying
to get up."

"You don't have to take my head off to
do it."

"Sorry, *Buck*."

Chandler said the nickname like he was
saying a rude word, but Buck let it go as he
climbed to his feet and watched Chandler
stalk off. Actually, Buck was Richard Cecil
Young, but that was only for his enrollment
card. Nobody at school or on the football
team addressed him that way: there he was
Buck Young. He looked more like a Buck,
rough looking, with wild black hair and dark
brown eyes. The name suited him.

The Tucker Tigers were in the midst of a
scrimmage, and everybody was pulling himself back to offensive and defensive teams
now, but Marshall was recovering kind of

slowly, so Buck waited to make sure he was all right. Marshall, the team funny guy, came across a little strange sometimes, but Buck couldn't help liking him. Easing himself up onto his knees, Marshall forgot about the football which lay in a mud puddle, and rubbed at the back of his head. Buck helped him up. "You okay?"

Marshall seemed shocked by the question. "Okay? No, but I'll live on to suffer these indignities bravely." He turned and limped away toward the offensive huddle, splashing and still complaining. "First my car, and now my neck. What's going to break on me next?"

Buck had to smile. He had been witness to the breakdown of Marshall's old self-help Chevrolet, the "Marsh Mobile." If Marshall was well enough to complain about that, then he was all right. Buck turned and jogged back to his own position.

"Nice one, Buck," commented Ray Burroughs as he rejoined the line. Ray was the biggest guy on the starting defense—the biggest guy on the team, in fact, and one of the biggest playing in the state. "Way to watch for that screen pass."

Buck felt good about the tackle and he laughed. "Marshall always gives himself away when he starts to giggle before the ball even gets thrown to him."

"Yeah, I've noticed, too."

The next play should have already been

set up and running, but there seemed to be a delay. Assistant Coach Dunheim was consulting with the offensive huddle, probably passing on some advice on how to run the next play. A chorus of voices was saying something or other to him, probably complaining about the rain. Buck didn't understand why. He almost preferred to practice—or play—in the rain and mud. It gave an extra edge to the game, the unsure footing presenting an additional challenge.

Inside his helmet, Buck's hair was dry, and he was happy, comfortable. No, more than comfortable. He was home. Although maybe not yet totally adjusted to this new school, the classes, or the different people, out here on the field he knew where he stood. And where he stood was near the midfield stripe, noticing that Coach Doc Samuels had just arrived, late today for some reason, and was now wandering up the sidelines, taking an acute interest in the series of downs they were playing.

"Let's go!" screamed Jim Grover, the right defensive tackle, slapping his hands together. "Let's hold 'em."

"Forget holding 'em," said Tony La Rico, the linebacker grunting behind Jim. "Let's concentrate on taking the ball *away* from them."

"What difference would that make?" asked Ray. Ray was playing noseguard. "They still get to be the offense. No matter

how well we do about taking the ball away
from them, they're always the offense.''

"Maybe we should complain about that,"
said Buck. "Tell Coach to give us the ball
one time and we'll run it right over those
yokels.''

"Yokels? What kind of word is that?''
teased Tony. "Another hick Midwest expression?''

"No," said Buck, "it's a big-city Midwest
expression.''

"I didn't know there were any big cities
in the Midwest.''

"Try telling that to someone in Chicago.''

"Let's go, let's go!" Coach Dunheim
walked away from the offensive huddle,
calling to the defense now and urging everybody on despite the rain. "Football is meant
to be played in the slime and the mud.
You're supposed to enjoy this.''

"Enjoy this?" said Ray. "I'm a barbarian.
I love this.''

"Rain makes the flowers and little football players grow," added Buck.

"Come on," laughed Dunheim, giving
Buck a friendly slap to the shoulder pads.
"Let's get these guys going.''

"Going all the time," agreed Buck as he
wiped his muddy hands across his wet jersey, leaving a brown smear. He walked with
Dunheim and Ray to the hastily forming defensive huddle. The guys there hunched
over, waiting for Dunheim's instructions.

Hidden beneath his blue baseball cap, Dunheim had curly blond hair and blue eyes, and Buck thought, except for the age difference, he looked like one of the guys instead of a coach.

"Okay, defense," said Dunheim. Rain dripped from the peak of his cap as he spoke. "I've heard you mumbling back here. The guys on the offense are letting the elements get to them, they're acting like girls because of a few drops of rain. I told them if they scored against the defense they could all go in early today. They said that would be easy, but I know you defensive guys don't care about a little rain. Do you?"

The guys looked at each other, and Buck felt the excitement rise in him again. Dunheim addressed a challenge to them. "Hold the offense against this drive, and you can pick one guy to switch places with Billy for a drive. He gets four downs as quarterback, and Billy plays defense." This was something Dunheim sometimes did, which Doc didn't like, but tolerated; a stunt to pump the energy level up. Normally it was good for laughs at least. "What do you say? Are you guys going to let this rain stop you?"

Ray snorted. "Rain? You talking about this Massachusetts mist?"

"It's just a little humidity," said Tony.

Coach Dunheim blew his whistle, and the defensive huddle broke with a "Tiger roar!'', and both sides started setting up at the line of scrimmage.

The play was a quick handoff to Hank Chandler, with Marshall, the wide receiver, supposedly leading as a blocker, but Buck and Ray deflected past Marshall. Buck was thinking about the smirk on Chandler's face as he and Ray caught him in a pincer movement, catching him from both sides in a tackle that Buck was pretty sure made the guy regret the day his mother met his father.

"Cover me," Buck heard Chandler groan to Marshall. "If you can distract the warden and the rest of the guards, I think I can make it to the wall."

"They'll shoot you like a dog," said Marshall, helping him up.

Hank grimaced, preparing to put his mouth protector back in. "I was afraid you'd say something like that."

The next huddle was fast, and in what seemed like seconds, sophomore starting quarterback Billy Tibbs was slapping his hands together. "Ready now! Let's be ready now!" Center Johnny Chappell took a firm grip on the ball, and Billy lined up close behind him, calling signals.

"Blue three! Blue three! Hut! Hut!"

Chappell snapped the ball to Billy perfectly, and Ray immediately clobbered him almost as perfectly, but Buck wasn't standing around to watch—he wanted in on the fun. Charging forward, he got thumped by Marshall coming off the line, but managed to knock the smaller junior aside. Twenty feet now, still charging. Billy was back, holding the ball with only one hand and scrambling to the right, searching for an open receiver. Ten feet to go now, and Billy saw Buck. There was panic in his eyes.

Billy paused, and in the pause Buck was all over him, but not in time. Billy's arm snapped like a mousetrap, and the ball rocketed away, just inches from Buck's face, and he felt it go by just before slamming his body across Billy's like a sack of potatoes tossed from the back of a speeding truck.

"Oomph!" was all Billy grunted before slamming back into the ground. Buck felt the "oomph!" himself, but it was all for nothing because the clapping and "All rights!" he was hearing meant only one thing: reception. Somebody on the offense caught the ball but, fortunately, had immediately been nailed by safety Norm Jackson, who came up to get him.

Oh, well. It was only about a seven-yard gain. There was always next play.

Grabbing a breath himself, Buck gave Billy a casual pat on the shoulder pads as he climbed off the quarterback. "Nice shot, *Kid*." Billy the Kid was a nickname Buck tagged Billy with early on in the season. Having been called by his own almost since birth,

Buck enjoyed tagging those around him with nicknames. "New handles," he called them.

Billy didn't seem too happy about being tackled; he slapped the hand on his shoulder away. It was Buck's seventh tackle or assist of the afternoon, and two of these had been on Billy, who was obviously none too happy about all the attention. He and Buck played two different brands of football.

"Sixty-six!" Buck jerked his head at hearing his number called; Doc was shouting over the rain from the sidelines, and Buck jogged over to see what he wanted.

"Nice hit last play," Doc said, "but the hit was a little late, and late hits mean penalties. I don't have to tell you what penalties mean, do I?" The coach waited, letting the question hang there, but Buck didn't say anything. He knew Doc came from the old school of hard-knocks football, and a lot of times he asked questions he didn't want answered. Sometimes someone would foolishly try to answer such a question, and then the real chewing-out session would begin. After waiting a second, Doc blew out a breath and seemed to relax some. "I like the aggressiveness, but maybe you should try turning down the volume on it. Okay? We don't want to lose our starting quarterback, and we don't want anyone else to lose their starting quarterbacks, either."

Buck swallowed, blinking to get some rain out of his eyes, not really understanding the

sudden attention. What was up? Buck liked
Billy; he sure wasn't trying to hurt him.
There was no way Buck was about to injure
Tucker's starting quarterback—or, like Doc
said, any team's starting quarterback. Buck
couldn't help being a little bit nervous. Doc
had complained about Buck's "overkill" before, but he'd never pulled him out of a
practice scrimmage to lecture him about it.
Aside from the head coach's position, there
was something unsettling about drawing Doc
Samuel's wrath. Maybe that was an asset; a
sense of menace always seemed to work
wonders on the football field.

Yeah, thought Buck. *Yeah, a sense of
menace.* So on the next play instead of turning the volume down, he cranked it up—
slamming into the ball carrier, fullback Chip
Moorehead, so hard that he nearly hurt himself. It would have been worth all the pain,
except Chip didn't go down, and there was
a grabbing of arms and legs and football. For
a few seconds it was like a mini wrestling
tournament: Buck wrestled at his last
school, and he knew that Chip was a state
runner-up in his weight class. Buck choked
in some air, his legs burning from exertion.
They both grappled, seeming to totter in
midair for just a second before gravity
worked again and tripped both of them
down, with linebacker Dan Hutchison
throwing himself on top for emphasis.

Chip was up in a second, rubbing at his

knee but grinning. "I almost ditched you, Buck. If it was just a little bit muddier out here, I would have been history."

Buck faked a jab at Chip's helmet. "Almost, huh? Almost only counts in horseshoes."

Chip laughed, leaving the ball at the line of scrimmage and jogging back to the offensive huddle. Buck liked Chip a lot; Moorehead knew how to take a hit.

The offense was lining up now. It was fourth down, their last opportunity to get in out of the rain, and they knew it. It was a battle of wills and physical strength and talent, but somehow Buck thought all the offense was worried about was getting in out of the rain.

"Hut!"

The play was a reverse, with the first halfback neatly accepting the ball—*pretending* to accept the ball actually—and taking off. The second halfback also passed the quarterback, racing forward, thinking Buck had been fooled, but needing to think again. Buck met this misguided individual just shy of the line of scrimmage, forcing a collison of pads and helmets with an intense smack, dragging the whole mess down into the slick mud and forcing a fumble. Now there was a scramble, and Buck found himself in the middle of a three-man sandwich, with the man on the bottom in definite possession of the football. It was Al Lucente, the luckiest guy on the offense in Buck's opinion, and he grunted, "Go ahead and stay up there, Buck. At least you're keeping me dry."

"Sorry," Buck crawled off and offered a hand up.

Al got to his feet and turned his facemask up to the rain, shaking his head. "I can't believe my mother lets me do this. I thought the woman loved me."

"You okay?"

Al shook his head. "You're built—and run—like a truck, Buck, but sometimes I wonder if the truck has any brakes." Al looked at Buck. "Don't you ever feel pain, man?"

Buck shrugged. "I feel pain."

"You just don't whine about it, huh?" Al wiped the sludge from the front of his jersey. "Hooray for football," he said dryly as he limped away, shaking his head. "My attorney will be in touch."

Buck watched Al leave the field, and he felt bad about it, but that was football. What the heck could you do? Tony and Ray were running over now, screaming taunts at the offense. "We took it away from you! Away! From you!"

"So who is it going to be?" asked Coach Dunheim as he came out on to the field. "Come on, let's go. Who's going to take Billy's place as quarterback for this drive?"

"Ray," suggested Tony.

"Yeah," agreed Norm Jackson, who had arrived to cast his vote before Ray could put up much objection. "I think Burroughs is our man."

Buck nodded and there seemed to be a general agreement. "Okay," Dunheim nodded. "But there's something you guys should know. The offense doesn't care about the rain any more than you guys do. The bet with them was that if they scored, Billy got to play defense and one of you wise guys *had* to play quarterback and get beat up for a while." The coach grinned, smacking Ray on the shoulders. "So I guess you guys either won or lost after all, depending on how you look at it. Go on, Ray, get over there and show us what you've got. Send Billy back as noseguard."

"No."

Everybody turned. This command was from Doc, and the tone of his voice made it clear that the *no* was non-negotiable. "I want Young over there," said Doc with a grim smile. He waved his clipboard in the general direction of the defensive unit. "Let's see how he appreciates getting slammed and tackled, again and again without mercy. I don't want anybody on the defense letting up. Play just like you've been playing all afternoon. But let's let *Buck* play quarterback for a while."

TWO

Jogging across the field, Buck tried to control the stupid grin he knew was spreading across his face. He'd taken part in offensive huddles many times before, but always as tackle—although at the first tryouts for the team he'd wanted to play fullback. Now here he was, casually jogging up, ready to play quarterback. The ultimate ego trip, every little kid's fantasy, although he'd probably wind up making a fool of himself.

As the huddle formed around center Johnny Chappell, Buck tried to think of a play to call, and he decided to ask the huddle. "So what do you guys think? What play should I call? What do you think we're up against here?"

That was a mistake. More than one guy

answered, "I think the defense on this team is a bunch of blood-hungry sharks."

"Wolverines."

"Vampires and werewolves."

"*And,*" said the first voice, "I think they're going to kill and eat the ball carrier on the next play just to show they mean business."

"Okay," Buck nodded, looking at them and thinking about it. "This next play is going to be a handoff."

A few guys laughed, and that broke some tension. There was even time for an editorial comment from Al, Buck's victim from the earlier fumble, who jogged up to rejoin the game. "Who's coaching today?" he asked. "Jacques Cousteau?"

Buck shook his head. "Welcome back, Al."

"What? You kidding? I wouldn't miss seeing you play quarterback for the world."

What was *that* supposed to mean?

Johnny Chappell was also shaking his head. "What have I been telling you guys? This is yet another sign that all is not well with the universe. Buck Young at quarterback."

Buck couldn't stop grinning, but nobody seemed to notice. He just kept shaking his head. "I just want to make it through this series of downs."

"Now you know how the rest of us feel," said Al. "Every time we see you over there, looking like some mad dog, all we're think-ing is, 'Lord, just let me make it through this series of downs, and I swear I'll never rob little old ladies again.'"

Marshall Danfield, whom Buck also slammed earlier in practice, returned to the huddle, greeting him with a slap to the shoulder pads. Marshall had another star-tling announcement as the huddle formed up. "I don't want to start any more ugly ru-mors, but there's this bearded guy behind the bleachers building this huge wooden boat—an ark, I think he called it—and he said something about hurrying up this drive because there's not much time and we need to round up some animals, two by two—"

"Right," said Al sarcastically.

"Really, though, Doc says to 'expedite,' and it'd be nice if we managed to score a touchdown."

"Right," said Buck even *more* sarcasti-cally.

"Just throw the ball to me, and you'll be all right." This was from Matt Kildare, who was nodding knowingly.

"Well," said Buck, "I was planning on running the right zero option."

"Right zero? What the heck is that?"

"I send you right, and you get zero."

There was some more laughter, but then Coach Dunheim's whistle blew, and the clock was running.

Buck swallowed. "Okay, let's try . . . uh, twenty-four right."

"Twenty-four, *right*?" asked Matt. Matt was playing on the left side, Marshall was on the right. Play twenty-four right had an option: the quarterback could either hand off to fullback Chip, or pass the ball away quickly to the right end, who would be waiting just across the line of scrimmage. And if Chip got the ball but had nowhere to run with it, he would also have a chance to throw it to Marshall before getting overwhelmed. Marshall was the safety-valve on the play.

"Yeah," said Buck. "Why not?"

"You sure you don't mean twenty-four *left*?"

Left would send all the action to Matt.

"We'll try that one later."

Matt shrugged. "Your loss."

Buck looked at the huddle. Time was running out now. "You guys ready to break?"

"Uh . . . Buck?" asked Johnny.

"Yeah?"

"What count do you want the ball snapped on?"

"Oh, yeah. Sorry. On one. Ready . . . Break!" Buck slapped his hands together, and the rest of the huddle did likewise in unison, pulling away to form up at the line of scrimmage.

Buck felt fairly ridiculous walking up there. Johnny was already hunched over the ball; the rest of the line was waiting for the quarterback to call the signals.

Buck swallowed, looking across Johnny at Ray. Ray was grinning at him, all teeth. It made Buck feel a little funny. He almost froze, but then remembered to yell. "Down!"

As a unit, all the guys on the line hunched over.

"Ready!"

The line came back up again as a unit. This was something Coach Dunheim emphasized, as it made the line formation look very professional to the fans and, to the other team, very scary. Buck yelled out "Set!" and the line went down again, this time into its three-point stance. Also, Dunheim said it didn't hurt to growl at this point.

Buck swallowed. All that was left now was to say "Hut", and the ball would be in his hands, and, no doubt, Ray would be in his lap—and he wouldn't be there to tell Buck what he wanted for Christmas.

"Hut!"

Snap!

The ball almost stung, it came back so fast, but Buck didn't drop it. There was an explosion of pads and grunting bodies all around him. Buck jumped back two steps, forgetting about Marshall who was crossing the line on the right and looking instead to his left, where Chip should be charging around. Where the heck was he? Where—

Ooomph! A defensive body slammed into his left side, and the concussion of impact drove the air out of his chest, and felt like it was snapping ribs, but Buck instinctively held on tight to the football as he started to fall. He didn't make it down before another body crashed into him, but there was no more air to drive out, and Buck just crunched into the ground. He could smell wet earth inches from his face, and it smelled good, easy, comfortable. He could relax there.

Except the whistle was blowing, the play was over. The guys were crawling off of him now, and Buck let go of the football, sucking in air, and struggling to get up. Buck managed to walk back to the huddle. Not a very impressive debut, he knew: it was a three-yard loss. Marshall greeted him by saying, "I was wide open."

Matt shook his head. "Marshall could have been in Boston and it wouldn't have mattered. Go left and get it off to me. You looked lost back there."

Buck looked at Chip who just shrugged in reply. Buck shook his head at the guys. "Quarterback sneak."

"*What?*"

It didn't seem like a popular move, but Buck said, "It's a safe running play; Doc likes running plays. Chip can walk me through the defense, can't you Chip?"

Chip grunted. "Absolutely."

"On two."

"Down!" he yelled when he was in position.

"Ready! Set! Hut! Hut!"

Snap! Buck had the ball and he gave Chip two seconds to get alongside him. Johnny Chappell pushed Ray off to the right, and this created a hole between the center and left guard which Chip and Buck immediately took advantage of. It was a pure power play, nothing fancy. It was just Chip and Buck crunching through the surprised defense. By the time Buck was brought down and the whistle blew, they had gained back the three lost yards and four and a half on top of that. It was third down, five and a half to go for the first.

Buck jogged back to the huddle. Tired and a bit battered, smeared with dirt and grass, soaked in sweat, Buck felt a tingling emptiness in his arms and legs. Cut and bruised, he was balling and opening his fists and noticed for the first time that the knuckles of his right hand had been scraped raw somehow.

For the next play Buck decided to try a typical Billy Tibbs option pass, but the protection wasn't there, and the defense read it perfectly. Buck had a good grip on the football, and he was scrambling to the right, slipping a little on the mud, but there was nobody free to throw the football to. Nobody. So Buck tucked the football between his arms and hunched low to the ground and started charging, running forward. He covered a lot of ground but he was running right at Norm Jackson, which was a mistake. Strong, toned, dark, and compact, Norm moved like a cat hopping tree branches. Norm was developing into one of the best linebackers in the conference. Buck was big, but Norm was absolutely great when it came to nailing a runner on the flat. Buck braced himself to give it a shot, but he didn't see Tony, who came in around the left end like a locomotive and caught Buck at mid-thigh, barreling across his body, blowing him back down by sheer force of impact.

Buck groaned a bit, getting up. This was wild. Why was it that playing quarterback was so much more physical than playing defensive end? Dripping with perspiration, Buck's heart was pounding, and the little twinges of cramps in his thighs and calves made him almost wobble. The most wild thing of all, though, was that they'd made the first down.

Back to the huddle. The guys were getting into it now.

"Here we go," said Buck, taking an extra breath. "I figure with this play I'm pretty much finished, whatever else happens. So let's make it count. Red Six."

Nobody disagreed. Red Six was the desperation play for when the team was down by less than six points and the clock was going to run out before another play could possibly be set up. "Only one problem," said Matt.

"What's that?"

"Can you throw the ball that far?"

Buck shook his head, "What? Are you crazy? I'll be tackled long before I get a chance to throw the ball."

Everybody laughed.

"I've got an idea," said Marshall.

"Yeah?"

"Call your signals different. You know how the defense always trains against the blocking dummy? Ready, set, *go*? No offense, Buck, but I think with your average defense man a certain amount of brain-rot has set in. I think maybe if you call your signals that way, somebody on the defense will think they should come across the line on 'go,' but none of us will have moved. That will totally throw them off. Johnny should snap the ball on the second 'go!' "

Buck said, "Why not? Let's do it. On second 'go!' Ready . . . Break!"

Last play. That's what Buck was thinking when he lined up behind Johnny. *This is my last play at QB, my last chance for glory.* "Down! Ready! Set!"

Everyone was in their three-point stance. The defense was primed. Buck almost grinned. "Go! *Go!*"

Marshall was right. On the first *go!* Ray and Marc Stapleton both jumped, felt instantly guilty, and hesitated. By then the play was running, and they were two steps behind. It was a blitz, with two linebackers coming in with the line, all of them hungry for Buck, but he didn't give them a chance. He hurled the ball away a full second before a blur of what seemed like the entire defense smashed into him.

"That smarts a little bit," said Buck when he crawled out of the pile-up, but he couldn't stop grinning.

Billy shook his head. "What the heck are you so happy about? You just got smeared. We almost knocked your helmet off."

Buck still had the smile on his face. "Touchdown," he said.

Max, Ray, and Billy all whirled around to see. Touchdown?

So it was.

THREE

On the field was where Buck felt at home. Here in the locker room, he couldn't quite make it work.

Who was he kidding? He didn't grow up here—most of these guys had known each other all their lives. He didn't belong here in Massachusetts, either at Tucker or on the team, despite the fact that he'd earned a starter's spot right away. He would have been better off in the army in Korea with the old man. Maybe that was the ticket: enlist and do tours of duty overseas with his father, rather than being shuffled off to stay with Dad's brother, his Uncle Vince, every time the old man got sent out of the country.

Buck was leaving the locker room when a

freshman stopped him and asked, "Wasn't Marty staying with you guys?"

Marty was a kid who'd stayed at Buck's uncle's house for a few weeks. His Uncle Vince and Aunt Amanda were Buck's guardians, and their house was always full. In addition to his cousin Valerie, his aunt and uncle were foster parents to kids with nowhere else to stay. Marty had been one of their wards. "Yeah," Buck nodded. "Marty was with us. So?"

"So nothing," said the freshman. He offered a pair of paperback books to Buck. "These were Marty's. Could you maybe get them back to him?"

Buck took the books and shrugged. "Sure, no problem."

Vince was waiting outside in a brand-new tan Chevy. Vince told Buck to call him by his first name, not "Uncle Vince," as Buck's strict father usually insisted when he was around. The Chevy had the itemized price sticker still in the passenger window and dealership license plates. Buck climbed into the front seat with him and nodded a greeting. Vince replied by asking, "Is that a friend of yours?" He was referring to Marshall, who was leaving the building, lugging his gym bag, starting the trek home.

Buck hesitated. He didn't feel comfortable calling anyone on the team a friend, really. He said, "That's Marshall Danfield."

"It's raining. Why don't you ask him if he needs a lift?"

Buck hesitated again. Vince was always trying to force him to make friends, no matter how uncomfortable or awkward the gesture might be, but he realized offering somebody a ride out of the rain was the civil thing to do. He rolled down the window. "Hey, Danfield!"

Marshall looked back.

"You in training for the Olympics, or do you want a ride home?"

Marshall walked over, looking embarrassed. "I live pretty far out of the way."

"We didn't ask that," said Vince. "We asked if you wanted a ride."

Marshall looked relieved and climbed into the backseat of the car. "Thanks."

"I'm Vince Young," said Buck's Uncle. "Vincent Young Chevrolet."

Marshall nodded. "Yeah."

Buck rolled his eyes. Vince was wearing his salesman smile now, and he started the car, saying, "I've got an idea. Why don't we all consider this a . . . test drive?"

Marshall nodded. "But I've already got a car."

"You hide it well," said Vince. So far it had been about a fifteen-minute ride out to Marshall's house.

"Marshall's car broke down," explained Buck. "He just needs to fix it up."

Vince laughed over his shoulder. "Well, don't ask Mr. Goodwrench here to help you," he said, sarcastically referring to

Buck. "I gave him an old junker off the lot, a sky blue Chevrolet Impala, absolutely free, and it's still sitting out in front of my house messing up the neighborhood."

"I'll get to it," said Buck.

"You keep saying that."

Buck tried to change the subject to avoid any arguments about the Impala. "You sell any cars today?"

"Oh, yes," Vince gloated, all teeth. "We moved a whole lot of iron today."

"I've seen you on TV," said Marshall from the backseat. "You're even better in person."

" 'Tell your mom, tell your dad, tell your rich uncle from Vermont,' " said Vince. He was quoting from his own television commercials.

They pulled off the road onto a gravel driveway which led up to a red-brick ranch-style house with a large yard. "Thanks for the ride," said Marshall as he climbed out of the car.

"Come on down to the lot," urged Vince again. "Credit is always easy to arrange."

"Thanks." Marshall waved again. He went up to his house.

Buck looked across the front seat at his uncle. "Do you always have to try and sell people your cars?"

"Good salesmanship is an art and a science," said Vince. He backed the car out of the driveway and started home, watching the road as he spoke. "You should think about salesmanship. Sell yourself. You're too shy around new people, you really are. How many friends have you got here in Tucker?"

Buck looked out the window.

"What about the guys on the team?"

Buck shrugged. "Games, practices. I see 'em in class at school."

"But are they your *friends*?" asked Vince. "Would they lend you fifty dollars if you needed it?"

"I don't think any of those guys have fifty dollars."

"You're missing my point," Vince said, "and my point is having confidence in yourself. That's where good salesmanship comes in. Salesmanship really helps you open up to people, which is great for the social life, if you know what I mean. As in 'talking to girls.' "

"What good would it do me to open up if every time I talk to a girl I'm trying to sell her a car?"

"Well," said Vince, "at least if she won't go out with you there's still a chance at a good sales commission."

Buck rolled his eyes. They finally got home, and Buck tried to ignore Vince when he gestured dramatically at the aging sky blue Chevy Impala which sat decaying in the driveway. Actually, Buck couldn't help thinking about Marshall's dead Marsh Mobile. That was an old Chevy as well, actually even a few years older than the one Vince had given him. Buck followed Vince inside and left his gym bag by the front door. Inside the living room he could hear his eleven-year-old cousin Valerie talking to somebody. Who?

Buck walked into the living room and saw Valerie and an older girl with shoulder-length straight black hair and wide, dark eyes. She was dressed casually in jeans and a peasant blouse and she sat on the edge of the ottoman, clutching a large straw beach purse to her chest.

"Say hello to Rachel," said Vince, who had already picked up the newspaper. "She'll be staying with us for a while."

"Rachel's sixteen," said Valerie. Valerie was all smiles.

Another foster child. Except this one was just about Buck's age, and a girl, which made him feel a little funny. "Yeah?"

"Rachel Tonachio," said Vince. "She's from Boston."

The girl didn't say anything, and Buck didn't know what to say besides "Hello."

Rachel nodded at him. "Hello back."

Buck's Aunt Amanda walked into the living room, sorting through a shoe box full of papers, and she said, "Buck, Mr. Boughamer from the movie theater called. He needs to know if you can sell popcorn a couple of nights this week for him."

Buck nodded. "I'll call him."

"You work at a movie theater?" asked Rachel.

Buck was almost surprised to hear her speak. From the reserved, tense way she was sitting he thought she was going to stay quiet all night. "Yeah," he said.

"Do you get into all the movies for free?"

"Yeah, usually," Buck nodded.

"That must be great."

Buck shrugged. "It's no big deal. We've only got one screen and the mall theater has four. They usually get all the good movies."

"Not true!" said Valerie. "You guys got *RoboCop*."

"Yeah . . ."

"And *Masters of the Universe*."

"Yeah."

"And—"

"Okay," Buck exclaimed, holding up a hand in defense. "We get some good movies."

"He gets me in free, too," said Valerie confidentially. "I get to go to the movies whenever I want."

"Oh, yeah?" Rachel whispered to Valerie. "Can he get us both in free sometime?"

"Sure." Valerie turned and looked at Buck expectantly.

Rachel was looking at him, too. There was something bright in her eyes that made Buck feel a little uncomfortable. He said, "I'll have to ask Mr. Boughamer."

Valerie took Rachel's left hand. "Come on," she said. "I'll show you our room—you're sleeping with me. She dragged Rachel up the stairs, and Buck went to call Mr. Boughamer. He needed help on Tuesday and Thursday. Buck looked around the corner to the kitchen where Vince and Amanda were fixing dinner. "Can I get a ride to work tomorrow and Thursday?"

"You could if you'd ever get out there and fix up the Impala," said Vince.

"Yes, no problem," said Amanda.

Buck told Mr. Boughamer there wouldn't be any problem, then he went upstairs to work on his homework before dinner. A while later, he was knee-deep in an algebra equation when he heard a small rap on the doorframe. It was Rachel, still clutching the purse, and her eyes were bright when she looked over her shoulder first, then whispered, "Are you a foster kid, too?"

"What?"

"These people obviously aren't your parents. I know the look in the eyes. I thought . . ."

Buck felt bad answering. She looked so lost. "No, Vince is my uncle, Valerie's my cousin. My dad's in the army, and I came to stay with Vince while Dad's overseas."

"Oh." She nodded, as if Buck had just passed her the secrets of the Orient. "Okay." She disappeared. Buck watched her go, then worked on algebra for another fifteen minutes before dinner.

At dinner, Aunt Amanda told Rachel that Buck was a football player, and Rachel didn't seem very interested,but it got Uncle Vince going on the subject.

"I saw some of practice," Vince said, "and I thought I was seeing things. Buck, what the heck were you doing playing quarterback?"

"It was just a joke," Buck answered. "Sort of a motivational thing."

Vince frowned. "Sounds strange, hard concept to sell. I don't know about this new coach . . . Samuels, is it?"

"Doc Samuels," said Buck. "And he's not new, he's been with the team since a week before they installed the dirt on the field. Remember, I'm the one who's new."

"Yeah, yeah." Vince dismissed this with a wave of his fork. "But I read the papers. This team hasn't had a winning season in years. Even that whiz-kid King didn't help them last year, and look what he's doing in college. He's tearing the Big Ten apart."

"Besides," Buck said, defending his head coach for some reason, "it wasn't even Doc's idea. It was Coach Dunheim's thing."

"Dunheim? Okay. So what's he like?"

"He's, like, an assistant coach. What can I say?"

Valerie spoke up. "I'm glad you don't come home bleeding anymore."

"Hear, hear," said Amanda.

Vince groaned. Valerie was talking about the stories she'd heard from Vince and Buck's dad, about Chicago football practices. Vince was agreeing. "That was a tough conference. But you think Chicago was bad? When I played football in Georgia, things were really rough . . ."

It was Buck's turn to say "Yeah, yeah. Coach Kowalski, yeah, I know."

"We've heard." Valerie was grinning.

Vince frowned. "Coach Kowalski was a great man. Just like your Coach Mekler, up in Chicago."

"Yeah," nodded Buck. "Coach Mekler was a great man. A great man and a great maniac."

"He taught you some good lessons. Just because you've changed teams doesn't mean you have to forget those lessons."

"Doc and Coach Dunheim say I need to cool my jets. The guys on the offense think I've got some kind of personal grudge against them."

"That's all well and good, you just don't forget what Coach Mekler taught you. That school had a winning season every year. *Every* year, just like we did in Georgia, when I played."

Buck found that funny to hear, considering Vince's constant speeches to him concerning confidence. Buck's last coach, Wayne Mekler, once told Buck, "Maybe you're lacking in talent, kid, but you can kick butt with the best of them. You'll do all right as long as you remember these three rules: Slam! Slam! *Slam!*''

Which was the problem Buck was having now. He couldn't forget those rules, and he was catching static about it.

There seemed to be a lot of those complaints. His own teammates were telling him to ease back. *Bogus*, was all Buck could think. What did they want from him? He did what he could do, no more and no less. Buck learned a long time ago to play his instincts. Usually that worked. After all, if you couldn't rely on yourself, then you really had no business doing anything at all in this world, much less playing football. Nobody in Chicago seemed to have any problems with his style—the whole conference had played like that.

I shouldn't be so surprised this is all coming to a head, though, thought Buck. *Welcome to northwestern Massachusetts,* he had told himself when he first got off the bus in downtown Tucker. *Please set your watch back twenty years.*

Throughout all of this, Rachel hadn't said anything. She did as dinner was winding down, though. She looked up suddenly and asked, ''Do you guys have a TV?''

''It's in the basement,'' said Valerie.

''In the family room,'' added Amanda.

"Can I watch some TV tonight?" asked Rachel.

"Sure," said Amanda, "but not too late, okay? We've got to get you a temporary enrollment at Tucker tomorrow.

"Can I watch TV with Rachel?" asked Valerie.

"For a little while," said Amanda. The two girls got up, and Rachel followed Valerie as she ran down to the basement.

"You guys watch channel twenty-one," Vince called after them. He had his salesman smile on again. "My commercials are on the movie tonight."

Buck followed Amanda and Vince into the kitchen, helping with the plates. He asked the question he hadn't meant to. "Why is she here?"

Amanda said, "I beg your pardon?"

"I don't mean anything by it. I just wondered what happened with Rachel to get her left in a foster home."

Amanda hesitated as if she wasn't going to answer, but then she sighed. "Don't make a big deal out of it, but her parents decided to get a divorce."

"So? Lots of people get divorced."

"Well, her mom went to Nevada for the divorce, and her dad went to Maine for some reason."

"And?"

Amanda looked sad. Even though she saw it all in her job as a social worker, she never became jaded. "And they both left Rachel in Boston, by herself, and neither one wanted to come back for her."

"Oh," said Buck. What could he say to that?

From downstairs, the sound of canned television laughter arose. *Family Ties* was on.

FOUR

"Okay, people," Mrs. Gilmore called things to order in English class, the last class of the day. Buck was sitting, as always, in the row closest to the windows. Mrs. Gilmore opened her attendance book and ran a finger through it. "Let's carry on with our oral reports. Who is next? Let's see. Ah, Danfield. Are you ready, Marshall?"

"Marshall *Danfield*?" asked a female voice. "What kind of a name is that?"

Buck cringed. It was Rachel. Buck didn't know if that was pure chance or if it was arranged that she be in his classes so she would see a familiar face. Whatever the case, here she was in his English class embarrassing him.

"That'll be enough," said Mrs. Gilmore to

no one in particular. "Let's make sure we give each speaker the respect you'll want when it's your own turn. Marshall?"

Marshall got up from his desk, carrying a stack of note cards. He looked terrified. *Why?* Buck wondered. Marshall was the most outgoing person he knew, always cutting up and telling jokes at practice. Now he looked totally out of place and out of character, with his curly blond hair and drawn angular face looking haunted. This only made Buck more worried about his own upcoming oral report; he wasn't the outgoing type that Danfield was, and if Marshall was this shaken up by public speaking, then Buck was doomed.

Unless . . . For a fleeting second Buck thought about Vince's repeated speeches on salesmanship. Was that something to consider? Was it really something that could be taught?

Marshall fumbled and almost dropped some of his cards before he started to speak. "Uh . . . My mythology oral report is on the phoenix. In the ancient Egyptian religion the phoenix represented the sun, which died each night and arose in the morning. Early Christian tradition adopted it as a symbol of immortality and resurrection. The phoenix represents something beautiful being reborn out of something horrible." Marshall cleared his throat and dropped his index cards.

"Then there is hope for all of us," interrupted Rachel.

The class laughed, and Mrs. Gilmore groaned, "Please . . ."

"I was just asking a question."

"Could you wait out in the hall please, Rachel?"

Rachel looked stunned. "What?"

"Could you go out and wait in the hall, please?"

Rachel got up, grabbing her books and big straw purse. "So sue me for asking a question. Sorry." She went out the open door to wait in the hall.

Mrs. Gilmore sighed. "Go ahead, Marshall."

"Uh . . . I'm finished."

Rachel stuck her head back in the door. "I don't believe I'm hearing this. I get kicked out of class for interrupting his report, and he was *finished*?"

Marshall looked really embarrassed, but Mrs. Gilmore just pointed a finger. Out, the finger declared. Rachel disappeared again. Next Buck felt Mrs. Gilmore looking at him. Why? Guilt by association, or what?

It was annoying. Buck tried to stay in the background in his classes. Life was easier that way. Rachel, on the other hand, was a loudmouth at school. At the house everyone seemed to like her a lot, she was so super-casual about everything. She called Valerie "Val," and Amanda "Mandy," and Vince

"Vinnie." Everything she did or said had to be different.

Ron Douglas's oral report was on the Pegasus, the winged horse, but Buck wasn't paying attention. Seeing Marshall, his teammate, up there had started him thinking about tonight's game with St. Augustine.

Buck was psyching himself up mentally, something which he felt was necessary in order to be prepared to spend two hours slamming your body against the irresistible force which was the opposing lineman. He couldn't help thinking back to his Chicago days and Coach Mekler.

Mekler said that for the first quarter of the game the punishment was almost fun— *almost*. The second quarter you played for revenge. You fought the third quarter out of loyalty for the team, but the fourth quarter, played through pain and exhaustion, had to be for yourself.

Buck didn't really pay as much attention as he should have to any of the other oral reports. He didn't really pay attention to anything until the bell rang and he heard Billy Tibbs teasing Marshall. "What about your car, Marsh? Think the Marsh Mobile'll rise from its own ashes?"

There was some laughter, but Marshall said, "That's not funny. I finally got it home, but if I don't get the car running I'm going to have to quit the football team."

Billy frowned. "Why?"

"I won't have any way to get home after practice or after games. I can't keep bumming rides forever."

Somebody saw Buck collecting his books and had an idea about what happened to the Marsh Mobile. "Maybe Buck tackled it while nobody was looking."

Buck didn't see who said it, and he didn't say anything.

Candice Tompkins and Sally Hoffman, both cheerleaders, showed some sympathy. They were leaving with Billy, but Candice waited and asked, "Can't you get a ride from your brother or something?"

"Are you kidding?" Marshall grimaced. "My brother hates me. He enjoys seeing me stranded."

Candice laughed and then looked around, waiting for Sally now, but Sally caught Buck by the door and asked a question. "Rachel is staying with you guys, isn't she?"

It was the second such question that week, and for some reason Buck felt twice as defensive about it. "Yeah. She's staying with my aunt and uncle."

"Why?"

"They're her foster family for a while."

"Oh."

Buck didn't really think anything of the conversation until he was sitting in a booth at the Arcadia Diner, killing time before the pre-game warm-up with an O.J. and his geography homework. That was when a small hand seized his collar from behind and gave him a surprise jerk back against the booth.

Buck pulled at his collar for air and jumped up from the booth, looking behind him to see what nut was attacking him. It was Rachel; she was leaning over from the booth behind his and she didn't seem happy. "What are you, crazy?" she demanded. "How come you told everybody I was a foster kid?"

"I didn't."

"You did so."

Buck remembered and got back his composure. "Well, I told one person, but I didn't tell everybody. I didn't know it was a secret."

"Who said it was a secret?" Rachel dropped back into her booth. She had a soda in a plastic cup sitting there, along with her well-guarded straw purse, and she took a sip. "I just don't want to give those people any more ammunition against me than they already have."

"Ammunition?"

"Yeah, this is like a war."

Buck frowned, looking around to see if anybody was watching them. Nobody was, but the clock on the wall indicated that it was almost time to start thinking about getting to the locker room. Rachel seemed pretty upset, though, and it was at least partially his fault. "What do you mean it's like a war?"

"People against people," said Rachel, looking around herself now. "It's like a war. Every time you move you have to battle all these cliques, all these snobs. It's almost impossible to make friends. You don't know what it's like moving all the time.''

Rachel seemed almost like a snob herself saying that, as if she were the only person to ever have trouble making friends. Buck almost laughed despite himself. He said, ''My dad's a master sergeant in the army. I could tell you all about moving, and then some. We've lived in California, Indiana, Chicago—''

''It's harder for girls,'' she said, cutting him off.

''Oh,'' Buck nodded. ''Right.'' He started to gather his stuff together.

''Where are you going?''

''To get ready for the game.''

''Oh, that's right, the football star.'' Rachel clearly had no interest in the game. She was looking across the restaurant to where some girls from school were gathering in a far booth. Buck recognized some of them from school. ''This is the way it works,'' said Rachel. ''Those girls have their own clique, so normally they wouldn't even talk to me. The trick is not to give them a choice, to just go over and start talking to them first.''

Buck though about Vince's salesmanship speeches. ''Is that the way it works?''

''Yeah.''

Rachel abandoned her soda and started to walk over to the booth. Buck didn't wait around to see how it turned out.

FIVE

Every time he descended into the dim light of the locker room, Buck felt as if he should be stopping by to clear out his stuff; that's how uncomfortable he felt there sometimes. John Bucek called a greeting, though, and Buck tried to pump himself up for the game. Bucek was still calling Buck "Mr. Quarterback." "Mr. Quarterback," he said, "I hear your sister Rachel is making a real name for herself."

Buck opened his locker. "She's not my sister, she's just staying with us." Remembering his conversation with Rachel, he added, "She's a friend of my aunt's."

"Oh, sorry," Bucek nodded. "I heard she was your sister. Anyway, I just wanted you to know I talked to her today in Mr. Lamb's class, and let me tell you, I *like* her attitude.''

Buck watched Bucek walk calmly away. Crazy. Bucek was serious, totally sincere, which made sense, Buck realized. True crazies always find each other.

Spike Crawford, a freshman back, walked by, trying to loosen up his left shoulder. ''Hey, Buck,'' he said, ''use your stuff on Paluso today. I'm still hurting from yesterday, so I know what you can do.''

Buck laughed. ''Football is a sport which absolutely requires a tried-and-true combination of analytical intellect and senseless violence.''

''You always say that, Buck.''

''So?''

''So,'' said Al, ''as long as I don't get hurt before Melissa Baumgartner from my algebra class agrees to go out with me.''

Buck blinked. ''Well? That's why we're all out here, isn't it?''

''To go out with girls from our algebra classes?'' asked Matt Kildare from the end of the row of lockers.

''To play some hard football,'' said Buck.

Ernie Howard was just about dressed. He was small, but moved fast, and would definitely be a contender for a starting position next year. He grimaced at Buck. ''You always play so hard?''

''In Chicago I had to play hard.''

Ernie grabbed his helmet, balancing it in

his palms. "This is Massachusetts, so take it easy."

Buck grinned, slamming shut his locker. "Absolutely never."

Al was ready to go now, and he just shook his head. "You guys can talk about what you want. We're going to need all our stuff together against Paluso. He's breaking records left and right."

"Yeah," agreed Matt Kildare. "The man is not lying. I read about Gordon Paluso in last week's paper."

"I think I saw that," said Dan. "What position does he play?"

"Back. Fullback, halfback, quarterback. You name it. He's like a one-man team."

"Then how come we've never heard of him before?" Ernie asked as he put on his helmet.

"He's a transfer student," said Al. "Just like Buck."

"Yeah," said Norm Jackson, taking the opportunity to change the subject. "A transfer student just like Buck and that crazy Rachel Tonachio. You got her in any of your classes? She's wild: she called Mr. Foreman a 'louse on the thick skin of mankind,' right in class."

"Ms. Fitch threatened to toss her out of economics," said Matt Kildare.

"Mrs. Gilmore *did* toss her out of English," added Brad Palmer.

Buck shook his head, slipping his shoulder

pads on, trying to keep a low profile on the matter. Coach Dunheim was stepping in now, calling out, "Let's expedite, gentlemen. You're not school heroes yet."

"Tell them about Gordon Paluso," said Al.

Dunheim thought about it. "He's definitely a threat. Probably one of the best athletes in the state of Massachusetts."

"I heard he's already been offered a scholarship to Notre Dame," Jim Grover, the two-way tackle, added.

"Don't drive yourselves crazy worrying about one guy," Coach Dunheim cut Jim off, his voice booming in the quieter-than-usual locker room. "Worry about the team as a whole." He pulled a scrap of paper from his windbreaker pocket and pulled his ball cap from his head. "O'Connor," he said, looking around. "Where the heck is O'Connor?"

"Over here," said Ted O'Connor, sticking his head out from behind a locker and raising his right hand.

"Lineup change, Ted. Pete Reiser's going to be really late tonight. You're starting at safety."

"You gotta be kidding," said Ted, a junior and one of the smallest guys on the team. He'd been taking his time about getting dressed, but this news caused him to hurry. He pulled himself out of his letter jacket. "Me starting on defense against this Paluso character?" he asked, repeating himself. "You have absolutely got to be kidding."

Coach Dunheim shook his head. "Gruesome fact of life: I never kid. Be ready."

Some guys slapped Ted on his back, congratulating him, but Ted looked nervous as he got dressed. He stared up at the ceiling and said, half jokingly "Thanks, Pete, thanks a lot."

"Pete knows better than to face Paluso," said John Bucek. "He probably won't show up at all."

Buck tried not to allow himself to get distracted by all of this. He was trying to prepare himself, and he couldn't help looking in the mirror and appreciating how the pads transformed him from Rich Young, transfer student, into Buck—a football monster.

Doc walked in and looked at them all. He'd obviously been listening, and he didn't sound too impressed with what he'd heard. "Gordon Paluso is *the* best, but that doesn't mean that he can't be stopped by a well-disciplined defense," he said. Doc consulted is ragged clipboard and made an announcement. "I've got the starting lineup here. Anybody fails to give me a hundred percent today, and you're more than welcome to watch the next game from the Tucker cheering section. So let's get out on the field now and act like we're ready to play some football. Move!"

* * *

Buck always felt a rush in his blood when he went out on the playing field. The crowd exploded into cheers when the Tucker Tigers charged onto the field. The cheerleaders were midway through a routine on the sideline, but even they broke it off to applaud. Billy Tibbs gave them a wave back, and then led the team through warm-ups.

Jeff Porter and Billy Tibbs went out for Tucker to meet the St. Augustine captains, but they lost the toss and came back to inform Doc they had to kick off.

Marshall, who did most of the kicking, cleared his throat and said, "Uh . . . I think my leg is sore."

"Fine, we'll have it whacked off after the game," said Dunheim. "Get out there and get ready."

"Yes, sir!"

Buck was part of the kicking team, and he followed Marshall and the others out. Across the field on the sidelines, St. Augustine didn't look like the threat they were being built up to be. They didn't have any more size or any more players than Tucker; the two teams seemed about evenly matched. Both usually wound up at the bottom of their divisions. Buck tried to guess which mulling figure over there was this "legendary" Paluso person everybody was talking about, but he didn't know the guy's number, and he couldn't tell otherwise.

The starting whistle came within seconds,

and then Buck knew who Gordon Paluso was. Marshall caught the ball wrong with his foot, and the kick came down short. The little back running under it could have called for a fair catch, and started St. Augustine with good field position, but he didn't. Instead he scrambled beneath the ball and caught it on the run. In an instant he was gone.

Taking a stutter step to his left, he evaded Norm Jackson and Ray Burroughs, who were nearly on him. The little guy was wearing number twenty-two, and Buck heard somebody screaming, "Double Deuce! Go Double Deuce!" and the next thing Buck knew, he was on a collision course with the little guy and closing fast. Chopping up clods of turf with his cleats, Buck reached and dived as the little guy squirmed by, twisting on his toes like a ballerina and sprinting from his grasp. Buck heard an odd sound as the guy flew by, and then he hit the ground fingertips first. He was shocked to feel that there was nothing pinned under him but air.

Buck tried to bounce back up to pursue, but it was too late. Ted O'Connor had missed his chance as well, and the whistle was already blowing behind them. The referee had his two arms straight up in the air. Touchdown.

Now Buck realized what the sound was he had heard from the runner. The little guy was giggling. Watching Paluso jog back to the raucous reception on the St. Augustine bench, Buck realized the little guy was having a great time at their expense.

"Touchdown return . . . ," reverberated the public-address system. "St. Augustine starting back Gordon Paluso . . ."

St. Augustine kicked the extra point with no difficulty, and John Bucek returned the St. Augustine kick-off to the Tucker forty-one-yard line before getting clobbered. Tucker was on offense now. Buck played both ways, so his role now was that of offensive tackle. *Time to take a few hits for Billy the Kid,* he thought as Billy Tibbs took the field. Now it was time to see what Billy had in mind for the night.

"Red Green Two," he said to the huddle, "unless they do what I'm afraid they might. I want to throw the ball short, but if I can't, you guys listen for the audible. On one. Ready . . . Break!"

All their hands slapped together in unison, and Buck felt proud as he stomped back up to the line of scrimmage. He felt it, and he believed it: he was part of a good football team. Maybe it could even become a great one. Too bad Dad wasn't here to see it.

"Blue . . . Four!" called Billy, "Blue . . . Four!"

That was purely planned distraction. The signal meant nothing, Billy might as well have been calling out instructions in Chinese.

"Hut!"

Buck crashed into the defensive tackle playing against him with a fierce clatter of shoulder plates and helmets. The guy was trying to shove him to the side, but Buck urged him back while trying to avoid the tendency to use his hands to keep a better edge. That was holding, and holding was a penalty. Doc and Coach Mekler from Chicago both preached the same line on that: penalties lose football games.

As always when he was on offense, Buck didn't see much of the play. But what did happen was he became aware of the fact that his right hand was throbbing, hurting. But not from this play. The pain was building. Buck looked at his fingers and shook his head. "I hate that," he said, jogging back to the huddle.

"What's that?" asked Marshall, jogging beside him now.

"Jammed fingers."

"Ouch."

Billy didn't take time to ask about jammed fingers. "Pocket pass on two, ready . . . Break!"

Buck walked back and waited for the down, ready, and set commands which came and were obeyed with threatening menace for the encroaching defense. Billy called out "Hut! *Hut*!" and the tackle across the line tried to take Buck's head off, climbing over him.

A padded knee caught him on the side of

his head, but Buck twisted out from under the tackle with some effort, and tried to slow the guy down some more, but now whistles were going crazy, and Buck heard a lot of groans behind him.

Fumble.

Buck grimaced. Tucker lost the ball and St. Augustine recovered, with really good field position.

"Oh . . . God," Buck heard somebody mumble.

"Time out!" screamed Ray. He had to scream it again before the ref got the clock stopped. Ray called a quick defensive huddle. "We gotta stop this Paluso kid."

"Sure," nodded back Matt Kildare, who was probably the guy in the best physical shape on the team, but always seemed to be breathing heavy during games. "What kind of rifle are you thinking about using?"

"I'm serious. He just got lucky on that return, and he's messing with our minds. It's too early to lose it. Stand the watch!"

All the guys threw their hands in a circle; Buck, too. "Stand the watch!"

Time in. Only their greatest fear wasn't realized. Paluso wasn't taking the field. He was being held back by his coach, and another player took the field. Tucker stopped the next St. Augustine play—a screen pass— by knocking the ball down, and Ray almost got lucky and caught it. Still, Paluso was not sent in.

"What the heck's going on?" asked Buck, shaking his still-throbbing hand as he set up on the line. "I wanted to get that guy for what he did to my hand."

"He didn't do that," said Ray. "You fell on it wrong."

"Same thing."

On the next play, St. Augustine gained a first down—even though Paluso was still missing from the St. Augustine backfield. Meanwhile, on the same play, Dunheim noticed Buck favoring his injured hand, and he sent in Dan Hutchison to replace him. Buck jogged off the field.

"Lemme see your hand," said Dunheim. He looked at the two red, swollen fingers and nodded "They're jammed, no biggie. Come over to the box."

They went over to the first-aid box. Dunheim taped Buck's throbbing index finger to his middle finger. "You want to sit out for a while?" Dunheim asked.

"Doesn't matter," said Buck. "I've played with worse."

"Yeah," nodded Dunheim, "I'll bet you have."

They walked over to stand beside Doc, and Buck asked, "What do you think the deal is with Paluso? He destroyed us, broke our momentum before we even had any, and they took him out. What do you think?"

Doc didn't say anything at first, and Buck almost turned to walk away, but then Doc said, "He's great, a terrific athlete, but he's a hot dog. That run was a fluke surprise. He got stupid with those stutter steps, he should have been nailed and he should have been hurt."

Buck nodded.

"Are you okay?" It was a dismissal of sorts.

Buck nodded again. Doc turned away.

"Okay, next play bring Dan out. Get in there and turn things around."

"You guys heard the man," Dunheim said.

St. Augustine had advanced to within easy field-goal range and was continuing its drive. Getting into position, Buck concentrated, trying to read the play before it was even a play. The ball was snapped and handed off to halfback Bill Kilroy, but Buck smeared him before he even reached the line of scrimmage, slamming into the guy so hard that he lost his mouth protector.

Now Gordon Paluso was sent back into the game, and Buck knew what they were thinking. Forget the field goal, St. Augustine was going for the score.

The next play Kilroy lined up opposite him again, apparently still a little shaken from Buck's tackle, but from the way his eyes were darting about, Buck knew that there was going to be no opportunity for Kilroy to redeem himself for the loss of his last play. This time the ball was going elsewhere.

Where? Far enough away to possibly allow for the defensive end to come in fast and sack the quarterback? Close enough to the line to make that kind of move a dangerous mistake? Where was the ball going?

"Red Fourteen! *Red* Fourteen! Hut! Hut! Hut!"

Incomplete pass. The defense was keying on Paluso, but they'd obviously expected it, and besides, it didn't seem to be doing much good.

Buck lined up to go again. His jammed fingers throbbed, but that didn't matter. The next play was wild, broken quickly, but there was a penalty against the defense—off sides—and the down was to be played over. When the ball was snapped it was handed directly to Paluso, who ran around the other end—away from Buck—and whipped off a pass just before he crossed the line of scrimmage. Ted nailed the receiver as soon as he caught the ball, but St. Augustine had gotten exactly what they wanted out of the play. It was now first down, less than fifteen yards to go for the score.

They were close now. Paluso was going for paydirt on the next play, Buck could feel it. The guy was going for the glory. The frustration of it all made Buck clench his fists, sending shivers of tension through his tired muscles. He had to nail this guy. He had to!

"Echo . . . One. Echo! *One!*"

The ball was snapped: the play was a screen pass to Paluso, who almost found an opening.

Almost.

Paluso was trapped between Ray and Tony, with Norm Jackson running up to assist, and that, Buck knew, was a world of hurt. It was going to be fourth down and they'd have to punt, only Paluso was—*what?*—slamming a palm down on Ray's back and swinging his legs out into the air. In a split second of admiration, Buck realized what was happening. Good God, Paluso was trying to vault over Norm like some Olympic gymnast on uneven parallel bars. Buck was almost there but he couldn't help feeling the anguish; Paluso was going to escape and have nothing but clear flat ground ahead of him. Buck was a failure, he'd let the guy go, he'd tried too hard and blew it.

Only he hadn't blown it. He slammed into Paluso while the running back was still airborne. Actually, he nearly missed Paluso but he did catch his legs while they were still flying. Buck throttled into them, and he was immediately buried, along with Paluso's legs, in a pile of defenders.

The loud crunch of pads and helmets made even Buck grimace.

Beneath the pile, Gordon Paluso wasn't giggling anymore. He was crying.

Buck got off the guy and looked at him closely. Gordon Paluso was a bright-eyed black kid, who still held onto the football despite his pain. He tried to choke back his tears, but it was obviously hard. Both head coaches were running on to the field now, along with the ambulance attendants who always stood by during the high-school games.

"Move out of the way, Buck," ordered Doc. The St. Augustine coach was leaning over to speak to Paluso while the ambulance attendants examined his legs. Buck was upset and confused. How the heck had this happened?

They had Paluso's helmet off now. He choked and said, "My legs, God, it's my legs . . ."

"You'll be all right."

"You were right, coach, you were right. . . ."

"Take it easy, Gordie," said the St. Augustine coach.

"Buck," ordered Doc, "get back to the bench. You're in the way."

Buck did what Doc told him; he always did. But before he moved out of earshot he heard the paramedics saying to each other, "I don't know, it's hard to tell out here, but both legs could well be broken. . . ."

No! Buck's mind screamed. He stopped in his tracks. *I didn't just break that guy's legs!*

"Buck!" Doc ordered again, in a voice that said this was the last time. "Get off the field!"

Buck turned and watched the sidelines and stands. All eyes seemed to be on him, but suddenly he felt very much alone. . . .

SIX

"Thirty-six to ten!" exclaimed Buck's boss, Mr. Boughamer. Short, thin, and with a very keyed-up personality, Mr. B was the manager of the State Theater, and also—in Buck's opinion—one of the nation's leading sports nuts. Mr. B could quote statistics for not only football, baseball, and basketball, but also ice hockey, college swim meets, international bowling competitions, and professional golf, just to name a few. He couldn't usually get to the high-school football games because they were played on Friday nights—the busiest night of his week—but he always managed to listen to them on the radio. Right now he was still going on about Tucker's victory over St. Augustine. "Thirty-six to ten," he exclaimed again. "Remember who said this first: This could well be the year the Tucker program comes back from the dead."

Buck shrugged. He was in the upstairs office filling out his time card, getting ready to spend his Saturday evening popping popcorn. "It was just an extra-conference game. More like a warm-up than anything else. I mean, it doesn't count in the standings."

"Warm-up game, huh?" Mr. B was running some box-office figures through his adding machine. The State Theater was playing a science-fiction movie called *The Greenhouse Effect*, and it wasn't doing too bad taking in money. Mr. B said, "I guess after that 'warm-up' game, and the way you nailed the great Gordon Paluso, they'll be calling you the Assassin instead of buck, huh?"

"I didn't mean to do that," said Buck. "I didn't mean to hurt him."

"How bad was he hurt?"

Buck shrugged. "At first they thought his legs were broken. . . ."

"Youse!" yelped Mr. B in sympathy.

"His legs weren't broken, though. I forget what they called it." Buck sighed. "I guess he's all right."

"What about you?" asked Mr. B. "They kept you out of the rest of the game. You aren't in trouble, are you? Was it a clean hit?"

"I *thought* so," said Buck. "I don't know

anymore. I keep thinking about it, replaying the whole thing in my mind. All I remember is everybody coming down on him. Norm, Ray, everybody. I slammed across Paluso's legs, and he started screaming and . . ." Buck let his voice trail off.

Mr. B looked up from the desk at him, and there was some concern in his eyes. "Are you sure you want to work tonight, Buck?"

"I'm okay," said Buck. "Besides," he added, putting his time card back in the rack, "I need the hours. I could use the money."

"Okay," nodded Mr. B. "Try to keep ahead of the crowd. We're going to be busy tonight."

That turned out to be true. The doors opened at six, and for forty-five minutes it was nonstop insanity. Mandy Baumgartner was working behind the counter with him, and she whispered, "I can't believe anybody would stand in line for half an hour to pay five dollars for a soda and a candy bar."

The movie started at seven, and things finally quieted down as the customers disappeared to settle down in their seats for the show. During the break from the mad rush, Mandy got out a bottle of window cleaner and started squirting down the counter glass. Buck refilled the bin with hot popcorn. Mandy was a year out of high school, and was trying to work her way through community college. She was also a beautiful blonde, and that made Buck nervous. She looked toward the lobby doors, where a line was already starting to form up for the nine-o'clock show. "Yo, Buck," she said. "We're looking at another sell-out."

Buck pointed to the small pile of popcorn in the bin. "I'm four up now. I can't make it go any faster."

"I know." She noticed the tape on Buck's hand. "Burn yourself?"

"No, I jammed my fingers last night at the game. They'll be all right."

"Yeah," she nodded, remembering. "You guys won big, right?"

"Yeah," answered Buck without enthusiasm. He was wondering, with a guilty feeling, how big they would have won if Gordon Paluso hadn't been knocked out of the game.

He tried to distract himself from the thought, and he asked a quiet question. "How busy does Amy look?" Amy Lowell was the cashier.

Mandy smiled. "She's on break. Why don't you go say hi to her."

"No time."

"You haven't had a break yet."

"I'm all right," said Buck, sorry he'd brought the subject up.

"Look," said Mandy. She put down the squirt bottle and paper towels and frowned at him. "You know you've got a thing for

Amy, and I know you've got a thing for Amy. If you don't talk to her pretty soon, I will.''

"No!' Buck almost jumped, but he held himself back. "Don't say anything to her," he said. But inside, he was half hoping Mandy would. That would be the easiest way: have Mandy find out whether or not Amy liked him. If she did, great. If not, then he was spared the embarrassment.

Mandy was smiling at Buck's discomfort. "I'm going to go on break, and when I get back you go on break yourself. And say hello to Amy." Mandy lifted the drop door and walked out from behind the counter and into the lobby.

Buck tried to concentrate on his work, but he couldn't stop thinking about Amy. On the football field he was brave, but when it came to girls, he was painfully shy. Why? Why be afraid of girls? He was as good as anyone, better than some. What was his problem?

For one thing, he'd never had a real date—although he was very happy to worship Amy, the curly-haired, soft-spoken cashier. Amy, a sophomore at Tucker, was also a would-be cheerleader. So she should probably like the fact that Buck was on the team. Right?

Buck got tired of trying to convince himself. Buck had been working up the nerve to ask Amy out for a long time, but he realized he'd probably never get around to it. By the time he worked up the nerve she'd be going with someone. That was the way it always worked.

Buck popped popcorn almost straight through the next twenty minutes, and Mandy came back from her break, egging him on. "Go on," she said. "Go talk to her."

Buck steeled himself. "Okay, I will."

"I'm serious."

"I know; I will. I'll talk to her."

And he did. He got out from behind the counter, walked straight to the box-office door and knocked twice, firmly. He stood there waiting.

Amy popped the door open and smiled brightly at him. There was a line at the box office waiting for her to start selling tickets that looked like it was a mile long. Amy's smile never wavered. "Yeah, Buck?"

Buck swallowed, then started fumbling in his pocket. "Uh . . . Got change for a dollar?"

"Sure."

Buck produced the bill and traded it for quarters. He used the change to drown his sorrows in a video game next door at the arcade. Maybe next weekend, he'd have the nerve to ask her out. . . .

SEVEN

Monday was cool, clear, and dry, and Buck went to school knowing it was going to be a great day for practice, but as he sat in his first class of the day—geography—he felt some of the same nervousness that he usually only felt on the field before games. Buck was surprised to find that he was no longer just a person at school, he was now a topic of conversation: everybody seemed to be talking about him, or to him, or not talking to him at all.

A lot of kids had questions about the accident with Paluso. Sports reporter Stan Flender had played up the events surrounding Gordon Paluso's injury in the newspaper, and now kids who hadn't even been to the game Friday held firm opinions about the incident, opinions they didn't mind spouting off before class. Buck almost got into a fist fight with an obnoxious freshman who was trying to impress some girls clustered near a row of lockers between classes. The freshman called Buck an animal, but he'd backed down when Buck stopped and called him on it.

But what if he hadn't backed down? Was Buck prepared to fight over what some stupid freshman said?

There seemed to be two groups spouting opposite opinions around school. The first and largest group was made up of people who accepted the fact that football was a rough sport where people inevitably got hurt playing the game. The second group was smaller, but more vocal, and strangely enough seemed led by quarterback Billy Tibbs. This group felt that Buck's usual recklessness had finally succeeded in getting someone hurt.

It felt like a stab in the back. Where was the team support when Buck really needed it? How come all of a sudden there were so many holier-than-thou sorts prancing around in shoulder pads?

Buck managed to make it through the day, but before practice he got called into the cage, where Doc and Coach Dunheim were waiting. Doc was seated behind his desk and he was blunt. "Sit down, Buck. We need to talk."

"There's a lot of ugly nonsense floating around this yard," said Doc. "Things were kind of worked up on Friday night, and I understand that. We're all calm now. I wonder if you could explain what happened during that play."

Buck swallowed. "I . . . I don't know. Not really. It was just like any other play, I thought. Except he was good. Really good. He was always in the air, it was like he could fly. Usually when you tackle somebody, you're going after their sense of balance. Just knock them awkward and they'll fall over. Paluso was never awkward, he always had his balance. Anyway, on that play I— we—just caught him while he was still in the air. I don't know what else happened."

Doc nodded. "That'd be about right, except for one thing. We've got a kid hurt now, a kid who maybe didn't have to be hurt."

Dunheim defended Buck, saying, "I don't think there was anything wrong with the hit, other than the fact that it wasn't necessary." He looked at Buck. "By the time you'd launched at him, Buck, Paluso was already going down."

"It didn't look that way on the field."

"Yeah, and I understand that."

Doc was blunt again. "I've been thinking about maybe having you sit out a few practices. Take some time to get your mind right."

That was crazy, and Buck felt his heart suddenly beating a thousand times a minute. "My mind is fine."

"We've talked about your . . . overzealousness before. I wonder what the problem might be."

Buck looked around. Why? Was he looking for help that wasn't there? "I didn't think I had a problem."

"Maybe we should all take time to figure it out."

That was when Principal Muscatini ambled into the locker room. Doc saw him come in and surprised Buck by muttering to Dunheim, "Terrific, this is just about all I need right now."

The principal nodded to some of the guys, making his way toward the cage. He rapped twice on the doorframe; Doc waved him in. Closing the door behind him, Muscatini nodded to everyone and said, "Good, everybody I need to talk to is here."

Buck blinked and swallowed. Waiting. Here it comes, and without any warning. It wasn't fair at all.

Principal Muscatini looked right at the head coach. "Doc, I've got a petition in my office, with almost forty names on it. It says that Buck Young should be kicked off the team for injuring Gordon Paluso last Friday. Now I don't know the whole story on that, but I've been talking to Principal Laughlin over at St. Augustine, and he thinks we might be able to defuse this whole situation before it gets out hand.''

Doc nodded. ''What are we talking about?''

Muscatini shrugged. ''I think that a short suspension might be a sound idea. Nothing permanent, but there is a lot of attention focusing on Buck, and I do have that petition. Maybe a cooling-off period is on order. A few weeks . . .''

Buck sighed, waiting for Doc to agree, but suddenly the head coach was annoyed. ''What do you mean, petition? Since when is my football team a democracy?''

Muscatini looked and sounded surprised. ''I don't mean to intrude in your running the team, Coach, I was only—''

Doc leaned forward at his desk. ''Nobody runs this football team but me. *Me*. Anybody who knows the game could see that Paluso kid was a hot dog. He was just an accident waiting to happen. This isn't a one-way street, you know. If you make yourself vulnerable to getting injured, it's only a matter of time before it happens. Those are the breaks.''

''But—''

''But nothing.'' Doc stood up, and Buck noticed that Dunheim was watching him with approval in his eyes. ''I'm not suspending a player who was just at the wrong place at the wrong time. If you want to suspend

Buck yourself, fine. But you better suspend me first.'' Doc waited.

Principal Muscatini held up his palm. ''Running the team *is* your business, Doc. But *you* run it. Keep this guy under control, okay?''

''Okay,'' nodded Doc. He looked at Buck, and there was something bright in his eyes. Buck could have sworn the man almost winked at him. ''Buck, you better get ready for practice.''

''Yes, sir.''

Noseguard Ray Burroughs was, fortunately, one of the people who seemed to have pretty much shrugged the incident off. At practice he set up right beside Buck as the linemen pushed the tackling sled while Coach Dunheim blew the count with his whistle. ''Bad bone bruises,'' said Ray. ''That's all I heard it was.''

Buck didn't say anything. He just slammed himself against the heavy sled and listened to the guys discuss things. A lot of people might have been surprised to hear it, but Buck found that linemen were generally the most philosophical guys on a football team.

''Hairline fracture,'' grunted Jim Grover. He slapped his fists together and shoved forward again.

''What?'' Ray took a breath.

Jim did the same. "I heard Paluso caught a hairline fracture in one of his legs."

"Hairline fracture?" chimed in Elwyn Brooks. Elwyn almost chuckled. "Where the heck did you hear that?"

"Around."

Elwyn slapped the sled's pads with extra effort. "Again with this 'around' guy. What—is he in your math class, or what?"

"A little less chatter and a little more sweat!" called Dunheim. He was pacing along behind them. His whistle shrilled, and they started pushing the sled again.

"How come Billy's so ticked off about it?" asked Elwyn. "It was just an accident. The way he's telling it around school you'd think it was Buck's fault he fell on the guy's legs. Sheesh . . ."

"It's not just Billy," said Ray. "There's a lot of clowns passing that around. Some of them are even on the team."

"I think they've just got it in for Buck," said Jim. "I'd swear Billy always has."

Buck listened to all of this as if he weren't even there. Finally he swallowed, saying something. "Maybe he just doesn't like linemen."

Ray laughed. "That'd be stupid. Those hotshot receivers may put him on the sports pages, but we keep him out of the emergency room."

"Or vice versa," teased Elwyn, twisting to look at Buck.

Coach Dunheim blew his whistle again, calling for a short break. Everybody got up and stretched, and Jim wheezed at Elwyn. "You're working out like an old woman today."

"Thanks," said Elwyn. "How old a woman?"

Amused, but feeling that he needed to get away from the banter, Buck moved over to the water jugs and away from Jim and Elwyn. Coach Dunheim pulled him aside for a minute, and he wasn't exactly happy. "Buck, I don't see much improvement with your moves. I thought you were making this a priority for me."

Buck felt uncomfortable. "I'm trying . . ."

"Trying is just a word, Buck. It isn't enough to hit hard. You've got to hit right."

Dunheim walked away from Buck, and Brad Palmer ambled over and stood beside him. He had his helmet off and wiped the sweat from his forehead. Buck expected another comment on his playing style, but Brad wasn't talking about football at all. "You got your oral report ready for English yet?" he asked, pouring himself a paper cup full of water from one of the jugs.

Buck shrugged, looking around. He was a little embarrassed to admit that he hadn't even thought about it, not with everything else that was going on. "I keep meaning to look at it, but . . ."

"Yeah, I know. Too much else to do."

Brad put his helmet back on. "Only problem is that it's due before the end of the week."

"Don't remind me."

The offense and special teams took a break about then as well, and Marshall came over to the water jugs, chattering to John Bucek and complaining about his car again. "Valve job? What the heck does that mean? The head mechanic sort of smirked at me and said 'total lack of compression.' Total lack of compassion is what I think. He's talking about an engine overhaul. He's talking about enough money to buy a new car."

"You could always take it to a vet," said Bucek.

"Why?"

"So you could have him put it to sleep."

"Funny." Marshall looked depressed now. "If I don't get that car fixed up, it looks like the Hopkins Central game could well be Marshall Danfield's last appearance with the team. And you guys know what that means."

Matt Kildare was there and he asked, "What does that mean?"

"Well," said Marshall, "obviously with my departure goes any chance you guys had of making either the championship game, or the Best Dressed Team in football listings."

A couple of guys laughed. Marshall noticed that Buck was standing there now, and aimed his barbs at him. "Buck, hey, glad to see you made bail."

Buck crushed the paper cup he was holding and tossed it aside, turning to walk away. He heard Marshall mutter behind him, "Sorry . . . what's the matter with him?"

Practice went on, breaking from offensive and defensive drills and going to a two-minute-warning scrimmage. Doc paced before the gathered boys and explained. "I think we're going to see a lot of close games this season. Don't pay any attention to that farce last Friday night. That accident had a lot to do with what happened out there afterward . . ."

Buck swallowed. Doc's attention was unnerving, especially since he knew the head coach was out on a limb for him.

Doc went on. "An event like that, a team's best player getting hurt, that sort of thing can't help but upset a team's momentum. But that was a freak occurrence which is not going to happen again, at least we all hope not." His look at Buck seemed to be saying, *Right*? Doc said, "A lot of our games are going to be decided by what we can, or cannot do, in the intense pressure of the final two minutes of play. Hence, these drills.

"The situation we're going to run is simple. For the offense, it's two minutes to go, with Tucker down six points. The opposition defense has so far completely shut down our passing game." He emphasized this statement with a look at Billy. "For the defense, we're trying to hold on to a three-point lead against a powerful offense capable of almost anything. It is first down, and the ball is at midfield. Let's see what you guys can do." He blew his whistle.

Buck took the field as part of the mythical defense. Since it was obvious Doc didn't want to see any risky passes, Buck got ready to choke off the run.

The offensive huddle broke, and the guys lined up against them. Buck was on the left defensive end and he found himself eye to eye with John Bucek. Bucek grunted and assumed his three-point stance on command.

The first several plays were routine, with Buck assisting on only one tackle. Billy Tibbs didn't attempt any passes, and the offense managed to get a couple of first downs. The clock was running down on the two-minute drill, though. On one of the final plays Billy tossed the ball out on a screen pass to Al Lucente, who then tried to run the ball through a gap on the end that John Bucek was creating by pin-blocking Buck.

Only Buck broke the block.

Slightly off balance and tripping at first, Buck quickly regained his step and charged right into Al, catching him from the left side and blowing him out and down across the chalked sideline. Al lost the ball, but only after he had gone out of bounds, so it was okay. He also got up very, very slowly and he asked for a replacement to be sent out on the field. Buck jogged back to the defensive huddle, feeling that every eye on the field was on him.

. What the heck was happening? He wasn't doing anything wrong. He wasn't *trying* to hurt anyone. But suddenly Buck felt very bad, because no matter what he did, he was going to wind up tossed from the team. It was ironic, wasn't it? He was probably too tough for their league. Now that he was finally good enough to play for Coach Mekler in Chicago, he was in the wrong conference, with the wrong players.

The first two-minute drill expired without a score. It was in the second two-minute drill that Billy Tibbs exploded.

Buck was almost on Billy, with Billy scrambling to get off a pass. Diving, Buck snared Billy's lower legs and brought him slamming down forward. The whistle was blown, and that was when Billy exploded. He dropped the football completely and jumped up, slapping his palms against Buck's chest. A crowd of players quickly gathered around them. Billy was hot, enraged, a madman. Tearing off his helmet, he pushed Buck again, roughly by the shoulders. "Hey! You!"

"Whoa!" Buck blocked Billy's push.

"What are you? Crazy? What's wrong with you?"

"What's wrong with *me*?" Buck blinked back at the quarterback, slightly amazed.

Buck tried not to allow himself to get worked up. He stepped back and jerked himself to the ready, but didn't react. Yet. "What?"

"What the hell do you think this is?"

"Football."

"That's right!" Billy tossed down his helmet. "And I'm on your team! We're all on your team! Al is on your team and now he's on the sidelines because you knocked him out of the scrimmage. Who or what the hell do you think you are?" Billy started to come forward.

"Hey," Buck held out his hand for the quarterback to keep his distance. "On this field I consider myself dangerous."

"That's the problem. You're a maniac."

"But I'm a football maniac, and all my hits are clean," said Buck. "The thing you're having problems with is the fact that out here I'm dangerous, but when I go down out of the locker room in my street clothes, I'm just Buck. You've got to learn that. Can you deal with that?"

Billy glared at him, not answering, and now Buck glared back. "I may play a little rougher than you're used to, but where I come from that's the way it's taught. And one more thing: We were also taught that what's started on the playing field, stays on the playing field. You're not supposed to preach about team stuff to your sophomore buddies in the school."

Billy didn't say anything. Not yet.

Whistles were blowing, and Doc was pushing his way through the crowd of players. He yelled, "If one punch gets thrown it means I've lost two players, because you'll both be off the team. Hey! Am I understood?"

Buck looked at Doc and nodded. Billy swallowed and said, "Yes, sir."

"That's it for today," said Doc. "Everybody take a lap and hit the showers. Take nice cool ones, understood?"

"Yes, sir."

Mumbling, the players started their lap. Buck trotted his, his heart again pounding from excited confusion. Billy Tibbs—mellow Billy Tibbs—had gone nuts on him. What next? How bad was this going to get before it got any better?

When he finished his lap, Buck slowed to a walk and found Coach Dunheim falling into step beside him. "Hey," he said, "I've got an idea how to work all of this out."

Buck looked at him. "I'm wide open to suggestions."

Dunheim nodded. "I know Coach Atherton over at St. Augustine pretty well, and I took the time to call him this afternoon. You should know that Gordon's going to be all right. He'll be playing again in a couple of weeks. And he wants you to come see him sometime." Buck was surprised to hear this. Dunheim nodded at him. "I think you should go."

"Why?"

"I don't know, really. Maybe just to see for yourself that everybody is making too much of this. When you believe that, maybe we can start changing you from being a good and tough player to a great, tough, and careful player."

Buck swallowed. "I never try to hurt anybody."

"Hey, I know that. But you've got to work on technique, Buck."

"You think I have to prove something to myself?"

"I don't know, you tell me," said Dunheim. "Do you have peace of mind?"

Buck sighed, shaking his head. "I just don't understand Tibbs. I always thought Billy was an all-right guy. . . ."

Dunheim frowned. "I wouldn't worry about Billy. This happens sometimes. It's the tension of the game. I think Billy just sees himself at the bottom of that pile, getting hurt himself, and that started him thinking."

Buck nodded.

Dunheim grinned now, giving Buck a pat on the back. "Remember, being a quarterback or even a coach doesn't make you perfect. Almost perfect, but not quite."

Buck laughed with Dunheim then, and they went into the noisy locker room together. Inside, Dunheim gave Buck Gordon Paluso's address, a place on Mulberry, and then Buck got cleaned up and headed home.

EIGHT

Rachel was sitting on the curb of the fire lane outside the theater when Buck came outside. It was about eight o'clock on Tuesday night and he'd just spent the previous two and half hours working the snack bar. His insides clinched a little when he saw Rachel. "What are you doing here?"

Rachel answered directly without looking back at Buck. "I'm watching that guy over there fight with his car."

Buck looked across the lot. Sure enough, there was a guy with his head buried deep under the hood of this stalled car, and a second glance confirmed for Buck that, sure enough, it was Marshall Danfield.

"Oh, terrific," muttered Buck. He sighed

another breath and said "Come on, Rachel.
I think I know this guy."

They walked across the mostly empty
parking lot. Marshall heard the approaching
footsteps and looked up. A look of relief
swept across his face. "Hey," he said.

"Hey, back," nodded Buck.

"Uh . . . About what I said at practice,
Buck . . ." Marshall was either very embarrassed or very nervous. "You know that was
all in fun. . . ."

Buck ignored him and instead asked,
"What have you done to that car now?"

Marshall swallowed and dropped his palm
on top of the grill. "I don't know. I thought
I had the Mobile running good enough to
come down to see the show, but now I think
it wants to have a word with a mechanic."

"What's wrong with the car?" asked Rachel.

Marshall turned to her and shrugged.
"Who knows. Nothing any of us could help.
They told me it needs an engine overhaul
for one thing. I . . . I fear the Marsh Mobile
has cranked its last."

Rachel stuck her head beneath the hood
and started fiddling with things. After a
couple of minutes, she said, "Try it."

"What?" Marshall blinked at her, confused.

"Get behind the wheel and try it."

Marshall looked at Buck. Buck shrugged,
saying, "What have you got to lose?"

Hesitating at first, Marshall walked around and climbed into the car. He cranked the ignition and the car sputtered, and then rumbled to life.

Rachel looked Buck dead in the eye, and her smile was almost chilling. "It . . . is . . . alive," she said.

"Where did you learn to do that?" asked Buck.

"I can do anything I want to."

"What?"

"My mom taught me how."

Buck just shook his head. "So what did you do to it?"

"That's for me to know and you guys to find out. It won't last, though. The guy's right, this car needs some serious work."

"That's great," called Marshall. He climbed out of the car and ran back around to the front. "I thought I was hoofing it for sure." He looked around before moving anywhere. "I need to get home before it dies again. You guys don't need a lift anywhere, do you?"

"Uh . . ." Buck hesitated. He looked at Rachel but she seemed bored now. "As a matter of fact, I usually walk, but yeah . . . we could take a ride."

Marshall grinned at them, saying, "No problem, climb on in. The Marsh Mobile delivers."

They all got in, with Buck up front by Marshall, and Rachel in the backseat. Marshall put the car in gear and roared out of the parking lot. "Take it easy," said Rachel. "It's just a quick fix."

"Sorry," said Marshall sheepishly. He slowed things down and turned on some music on the car radio. He looked across the seat at Buck. "You've got your own junker at home, right?"

Buck shrugged, thinking about it. "Yeah. It's a real pain to mess with, though. I haven't even bothered to do anything with it yet. I've got other things to do, you know?"

"Yeah," nodded Marshall. Then he asked, "Is your uncle really as crazy as he seems on television?"

"You saw for yourself," said Buck. "He's a lot worse."

Marshall looked back at Rachel. "And you're staying with them? With Crazy Vince?"

"Yeah," answered Rachel dryly. "I have that privilege."

"Are you guys related or something? You and Buck?"

"Or something," said Buck.

"What?"

Rachel was laughing. "I'm Buck's sister."

Buck quickly looked back at her. Marshall seemed confused. "I heard that, but then . . ." He looked at Buck. "You said that wasn't true."

"I embarrass Buck sometimes, but I am definitely his sister," continued Rachel.

"I've been away at private school—in Switzerland no less—and we haven't seen each other in absolutely *ages*, but there you go."

"Wow," said Marshall. "Private school in Switzerland. That's weird."

"Just what I was thinking," said Buck.

Rachel was quiet for a minute, seeming to work up to something and then she said, "You know, Buck, I was thinking. You remember Marshall's report in English class?"

"No."

"Sure you do. The phoenix, the bird reborn from ashes. Your car is a Chevy, too, right? So why couldn't we do a phoenix with both cars?"

Buck gave Marshall an odd, questioning look. Marshall just shrugged. He didn't know what was going on, either.

Rachel went on. "This car is on its last legs, and heck, your junker isn't even running. We could probably use parts from both cars to put one really good one together."

Marshall interrupted, clearing his throat. "Uh . . . I don't know . . ."

"It'd be great."

"Great for you," said Buck, "but it sounds like I'm out a car."

Rachel was all excited, caught up in her idea. "No, no. You guys could share. Take turns with it."

Buck looked at her. "Sounds like a stupid idea."

"Why?"

Buck looked at Marshall. "You tell her, Marsh."

Marsh just shrugged. "I can't think of any reason not to at least think about it."

Buck felt his temper flare. "Because I don't know anything about cars, okay? That's why I haven't fixed up the stupid junker Vince gave me. Okay? Is that such a big deal? I'm not mechanically inclined. Is that a crime, or what?"

Marshall hesitated a second. "Well, heck, Buck. I don't know that much, either, but I figured from the way she was talking we'd get your sister here to do all the work."

Rachel started to laugh in the backseat. "Why not? I'd do anything for the privilege of watching you two clowns work together."

"See?" said Marshall. "All we have to do is keep her entertained."

Buck couldn't help but laugh at that. The idea was a little tempting, though, if for no other reason than it would keep Rachel busy for a while and out of his hair.

They were passing Mulberry Road now. Buck remembered the address Dunheim had given him and said, "Maybe. You'll have to give me time to think about it, though. Pull down Mulberry Road."

"What?"

"Come on, just do it."

Marshall made the turn. The lights from

the houses on both sides of the road illuminated the street. "What's up?"

"We're in the neighborhood. I thought we could go see somebody."

"Who?"

"Gordon Paluso."

Marshall looked straight at Buck. "Say *what*? Are you crazy?"

"I'll let you know in a few minutes. There's the number, pull into the driveway here." Buck pointed to a large red brick house.

Marshall pulled in behind a parked station wagon. Buck got out of the car, walked up to the house alone, and rang the bell. A big black man answered the door, carrying the remains of a newspaper. "Can I help you, son?" he asked.

"Uh . . . is this the Paluso residence?"

"That it is; I'm Mr. Paluso. And? . . ."

Buck swallowed. "Is Gordon around?"

Mr. Paluso nodded. "He sure is. Can I tell him who's here?"

Buck swallowed again, now feeling very uncomfortable about the whole thing. "Buck Young. Coach Dunheim at Tucker said Gordon wanted me to stop by. I . . . I'm the guy who tackled him at the game."

Mr. Paluso nodded. "Oh. Well. Then I guess you'd better come on inside."

Buck followed him into the living room, which looked comfortable and expensive, and Mr. Paluso called to his son. "Gordie!"

"Yo!" answered a voice from upstairs.

"You've got a visitor."

"Male or female?"

Mr. Paluso laughed. "Mr. Romance, it's the guy who tackled you Friday."

"Oh," answered the voice. "Send him on up."

Mr. Paluso pointed the way, and Buck went up the stairs. Gordon's room was the first on the right, and the door was open. Buck recognized the face as the same one grimacing inside his helmet Friday night, the same one giggling as he made that great touchdown return. Now he was seated in a chair, hunched over a large drafting board, drawing something. A pair of crutches stood against the wall, but there were no horrible-looking casts on Gordon's legs. Buck stepped into the doorway and saw that he was drawing cartoons. Large kangaroo characters in three colors. Not bad, either. Really good in fact. Buck stood there a few seconds and cleared his throat.

"Oh, sorry," Gordon turned around. "I get kind of involved. Come on in, Buck."

"You . . . you know me, huh?"

"Oh, yeah." Gordon grinned at him. "Coach Atherton had Tucker scouted and he told us before game day to watch for Billy Tibbs's passes, and big Buck Young on the defense. Coach was real worried about you."

Buck didn't know whether to be embarrassed or flattered. "Really?"

"I kid you not."

"Uh . . . I guess that's good," said Buck. He laughed and said, "You know, you almost ran us off the field all by yourself."

"Yeah? Well, that's the way to play, I guess. You hit and I run, right?"

"Right. I'm sorry about you getting hurt, though."

"Yeah, well . . . it was a lot my own fault," said Gordon. "That's absolutely true. Coach Atherton and my dad kept telling me if I continued trying that Superman single-bound flying-leap stuff, I was going to get my fool legs broken. Which I almost did," he laughed.

Gordon replaced the cap on one of his drawing pens. "I think I got off lucky. Just some heavy bruises. I'll be playing again in a couple of weeks, and in the meantime I get to spend more time drawing. That's what I want to do, you know, really. Anybody can play football, but how many people do you know with their own comic strips?"

"Not a one."

"Absolutely."

Buck was still embarrassed about one thing. "A lot of people—guys on the team, even—they think I play too rough, that's why you got hurt."

"What? You kidding?" Gordon laughed. "This conference is kind of mild mannered. The team I used to play on always had guys out for injury. That's the way it was, tough league."

"Yeah? Where did you play?"

"Chicago."

"Yeah?" Now Buck couldn't help but smile. "Which conference?"

"Triple A South Central. You know it?"

"Know it? I used to play for Grant."

"Hardcore Grant?"

"That's the one," said Buck.

Gordon started laughing. "I can't believe that. Well, now we know where you learned to play ball, anyway. I was over at Wheating before my Dad got the job out here and we all moved. He was sick of the public-school system, though, so I wound up at St. Augustine. Otherwise, us two Chicago boys might be playing together instead of against each other."

"Yeah," nodded Buck. He noticed the time and started to leave. "Thanks. I wanted to stop by."

"Glad you did," said Gordon. "And forget the football. If you ever need any serious cartooning done, though, come and see me first. Okay?"

"That I will," said Buck. He left Gordon at his drafting board and ran downstairs and outside to tell Rachel and Marshall his decision on Rachel's phoenix car project.

Rachel nodded, not saying anything. Marshall's reaction was two words: "All right!"

NINE

English class. Buck knew he was running out of people who were ahead of him to give their reports, but he hadn't realized how close to judgment he was. Before class some people were slinking around, talking about their oral reports, and Rachel, who was probably not even going to have to do one of her own, elbowed him on the sly. "Hey, Mr. Football. Got your report ready?"

Buck shook his head. "No time. I keep meaning to get something together, but what with work, the team, this mess with Gordon Paluso, and now the deal with Marshall about the cars . . . who's got time?"

"Could get ugly," said Rachel.

Buck shook his head. "Nah, I should have a few more days."

Or so he had assumed until Mrs. Gilmore started class by opening her attendance book and announcing "Okay, let's see about our mythology oral reports today: Palmer, Tressey, Vangelder, and *Young*."

Buck was sure the gulp he swallowed was heard in the girls' gym class, halfway across the school campus.

Mrs. Gilmore double-checked her list. "Oh, and Tonachio. Rachel?"

Rachel looked up, pushing her bangs out of her eyes, and Buck saw she had an odd smile on her face. "Yes, ma'am?"

"Did you have a chance to prepare some material for a mythology oral report? I know you didn't have as much time as the rest of the class and—"

Rachel smiled confidently. "I'm always ready."

"Great," nodded Mrs. Gilmore. "Let's get started."

Brad Palmer was first up, and Buck tried to make himself disappear from view. He hunched low in his desk, praying for a reprieve. Brad's report was absolutely brilliant. He hardly even glanced at his note cards, speaking in a casual way about Icarus and Daedalus, the father and son from Greece who flew out of jail by making a pair of wings from gull feathers and wax. Icarus flew to close to the sun, though, and his wings melted.

Brad took ten minutes, and Sylvia Tressey

was next. She was almost as good, talking about the Minotaur, who was half-man, half-bull, and when she was finished there were thirty minutes left in the class period. Then Angie Vangelder got up, and Buck knew he had a chance—a remote chance—because Angie always droned on and on about things, and today she had a subject she obviously knew a lot about: the end of the Trojan War and the voyage home of Ulysses.

Mrs. Gilmore settled back into her seat for this one, making notes with her pen, and Buck crossed his fingers. Angie would probably go on forever, leaving nobody else with any time. But she didn't; she spoke for just over twelve minutes, leaving plenty of time for Buck to make a complete idiot of himself.

Mrs. Gilmore scanned her list. "Young," she said. "You may begin whenever you're ready—"

Suddenly Rachel interrupted. "Hey," she said.

Mrs. Gilmore looked up from her notepad. "Yes, Miss Tonachio?"

"What about me? I thought you were going alphabetically, but then you let Angie go before me."

"Well, I only thought you'd want the time—"

"I've been ready for a long time, and you're going to run out of time for me."

"We can get to you tomorrow, Rachel."

"Hey, that's not fair. It's my turn, isn't it?"

Mrs. Gilmore hesitated. She glanced over at Buck. "Would you mind?"

Buck waved his hands back, feeling relief wash over him. He tried not to give himself away, but he felt like he'd looked into the valley of death and been pulled back by a friendly pair of arms. "It's all right with me."

"Great. Rachel?"

Rachel got up and walked to the front of the classroom. She didn't have any notes at all, and it was pretty obvious she had no idea what it was she was going to say. "I sort of remember this story," she said, "maybe it was a movie I saw on TV or something. I think it was myth stuff. This lady, who was like Mother Nature, she had this beautiful daughter, and the god of the underworld fell in love with her, and that's how come we have winter. Different seasons, I mean. See, he wanted to marry her . . ."

Rachel babbled on for a full ten minutes and to everybody else in the class she must have looked ridiculous. Buck realized what she was doing, though, and he didn't know what to think, or to say. When Rachel was finished the class started chuckling, mocking Rachel and asking her to repeat, "Whatever it was you just said." Mrs. Gilmore just shook her head sadly, marking down Rach-

el's grade, and then she announced that
Buck would have to give his report the next
day. Rachel made her way slowly back to
her seat, being quietly teased by the kids
around her, and as she passed Buck she just
shrugged. "What's a sister for, huh?"

Yeah, Buck thought then and now in the
locker room, getting ready for practice.
What's a sister for?

Pulling on his cleats, Buck realized—oddly
enough—that as difficult as it was for him
to believe, he was actually starting to miss
Chicago. He even missed Grant and Coach
Mekler, although he'd been forced to grow
up very fast in that type of school. There
was one thing to say for the place, though.
At least there he always knew where he
stood.

Here at Tucker, it seemed like nobody was
consistent. Rachel was the absolute, ultimate wild card. Billy Tibbs went from mellow quarterback to screaming maniac, and
now Buck noticed that even Marshall Danfield was showing his other side. The night
before he'd been all worked up over the idea
of molding their two cars into one, and Buck
had expected Marshall to be yapping on the
subject a mile a minute. It wasn't happening, though. Marshall usually babbled and
joked about something or other, but today
he was quietly getting dressed just like the
others, and Buck just shook his head si-
lently. He was even more confused when

Marshall finished dressing and stood up on one of the benches, his helmet in his hands. He looked as if he were going to make one of Jeff Porter's pre-game speeches.

Not exactly. The rest of the team was close to being ready to go out onto the field when Marshall started speaking. He cleared his throat and said, "The line of talk going on is kind of ignorant."

Not that many guys were listening; they continued snapping up helmets and lacing up cleats.

"Hey!" Marshall let his helmet fall and bounce off the concrete floor like a basketball. Crack! Now everybody was watching him. He said "I'm serious. If they were going to clone idiots, a lot of you guys would be great for donor tissue."

Buck looked around. He noticed Billy Tibbs and some of the freshmen were watching Marshall very closely. Some of the older guys looked more shocked, offended. Was anybody going to make a move? Terrific. In a second Buck knew he was going to wind up in a fight, sticking up for a Marshall Danfield, who had gone off the deep end, and they were definitely going to have a reason to kick him off the team. Terrific.

Marshall started speaking. "This is really bothering me, and I hate to be a spokesman, but somebody has to, and our usual candidates won't speak."

Elwyn Brooks said, "Jim's running for

Student Council. Let him make the speeches.''

"Quiet," said Jim. "Go on ahead, Marsh. What's on your mind?"

"Buck Young."

The subject of all the attention, Buck swallowed and tried not to feel all the eyes that must have been staring at his back.

Marshall went on. "I'm talking about the accident with Gordon Paluso. Somebody in my third period tried to get me to sign a petition against Buck. Gordon Paluso isn't being stupid about the accident, but a lot of the guys here are. We all know Buck didn't hurt anybody on purpose, and I think it's time we start telling everybody else. We're Buck's teammates and we should stick by him. Sometimes Buck doesn't know his own strength, granted, but heck, sometimes Ray doesn't know his own intellect, and sometimes I don't fully understand the attraction, the devastating animal magnetism I display for women. . . ."

Somebody called out, "Airborne assault!" just then, and that was the end of the speech. Socks bombarded Marshall from all directions, bouncing off him and falling to the floor. Except for the pair that Doc caught. He just shook his head, bewildered as always by locker-room humor, and said, "Just get out on the field."

Everybody listened. Out on the field, they'd been scrimmaging for less than fif-

teen minutes before Buck caught a block
wrong and got smeared. He'd been smeared
a few times before, and each time Coach
Dunheim chewed him out for some error in
technique, but this time he was trying to
trap Jim Grover between himself and center
Johnny Chappel when he lost his footing.
Before he could regain anything Jim was
running right over him, plowing him down
into the ground. His helmet was jarred loose,
and in a split second of sudden pain he felt
his nose smashed against his face, blood suddenly gushing from it.

Well, this was interesting, Buck thought.
He got up slowly, pulling his helmet off his
battered face. Salty-tasting blood was running across his lips and at the same time
down the back of his throat. His nose was
bleeding like a stuck pig, which was to say
a lot.

Coach Dunheim was no help. He raced
over from the sidelines and said, "Well,
Buck, I'm afraid that was coming for a long
time."

Buck leaned his head back and held a
bloody hand beneath his nose, trying to ap-
ply pressure. It didn't really hurt, it was just
bleeding; so his nose probably wasn't broken. He rolled his eyes at the coach and said,
"Say what?"

Dunheim gave him a damp cloth. "That
trap block, Buck. You try to use your power
to overcome your poor technique, and it was

only a matter of time before you got splattered.''

"Poor technique?" Buck swallowed. His voice sounded funny with him holding his nose like this. "So why didn't you say so before?"

"I did say so before. You never listen."

Buck didn't say anything. It was true.

Dunheim cocked his head. "So are you ready to listen now?"

Buck moved the blood-soaked rag away from his face. The back of his throat still tasted bitter and salty, but the bleeding had pretty much stopped. He sighed, feeling almost tired. "Am I good enough to play, or what? I don't want to be a problem. Do you guys want me here or not?"

Dunheim frowned. "Of course we do. I wouldn't waste my time if there wasn't talent or potential to develop. But you've got to know that there's always room for improvement." Dunheim grinned now, saying, "Buck, you have the ability to be absolutely amazing. And sometimes I think you forget that takes work and sweat—a lot of it, all the time."

Buck thought a second. "I'm not sure what all that means."

Dunheim hesitated only a few seconds. "Do you want to play football?"

"Yeah," Buck said. "Let's do it."

Back in scrimmage play, Buck worked like a madman. Often a play went wrong, and

Dunheim would point out a technical error. He was very big on penalties, pointing out the slightest holding or pass interference incidents. The frustrations mounted, the pressure was high, but Buck thought Dunheim was intentionally trying to push him and in a way that was flattering. He spent the practice trying to think less about the Chicago ways of doing things, and more about Doc and Dunheim and Tucker and this new scheme of things.

Buck still hit and tackled just as hard. But eventually Dunheim started to nod instead of complain. You couldn't rework a style of play in an afternoon or a week, but it was definitely a start. And one thing was happening. Buck was starting to master the movements of the trap, with Coach Dunheim teaching him the moves. Buck realized that the details had been told to him a number of times, but he'd never really paid attention. It was easier to excel with Coach Mekler's thunder-on-cleats philosophy than it was to try and adjust to a team style.

Doc's whistle blew and it was time for a break. Buck had never felt this worn out at practice before, and he dragged himself toward the water jugs for a drink. He had to wait in line, and while he was standing there Matt Kildare sort of chuckled at him. "What's this lunacy I hear about you and Marshall Danfield playing General Motors?"

Buck reached for a paper cup full of water. He didn't even get to answer before Marshall was there, grinning. "It's true, absolutely true," he said. "Buck and I are building a car together."

"Out of what? Play-dough?"

"No, out of his old junker and my old junker. It's like the phoenix, you know? Out of the ashes . . ."

Matt shook his head. "Yeah, yeah . . ."

"This is going to be great. You all wait and see."

"I don't know," said Matt doubtfully. "Any mechanical project involving Buck Young and Marshall Danfield has got to be a circus. I doubt you guys could put together a model car, much less a real one."

Marshall hesitated only an instant. "I'll bet you we'll be rolling by Friday night's game. We'll be cruising in our new car right after the game."

Matt snorted. "Hah! I'll bet you pizza for the team that you won't even be able to drive the thing to the mall and back."

"You're on!" said Marshall instantly.

"Great," said Matt. "I'll spread the word. Danfield the pedestrian is buying pizza after the game Friday."

Buck swallowed his water and spoke quietly to Marshall. "Uh . . . Danfield, maybe . . ."

"Relax," said Marshall, very cocky. "I've got this well in hand."

"Marsh, we haven't even started on the car yet."

"So how long can it take?"

"I haven't the slightest idea. That's what worries me."

"I'm not worried. Rachel will come through for us."

Buck hated to admit that he was starting to believe in Rachel himself; he was too cynical for all that, wasn't he? He pointed out that "All Rachel did was start your car. Or so we think—that may have even been a coincidence. We don't know how much she knows about mechanics."

Marshall said again, "I'm not worried."

"Okay," nodded Buck. "Have you considered how much pizza for this entire team is going to cost? Think about Jim Grover and Elwyn Brooks alone; they call them the Pepperoni Twins. And I'm going to add just two more words to that: Ray Burroughs."

Marshall thought about it. Buck knew he was now seeing an endless sea of pizzas being rung up by smiling cashiers and handed to Big Ray, who then casually sucked them down. Marshall's face paled a bit. "Okay," he said, "now I'm worried."

"Terrific, I feel so much better." Buck just shook his head. Doc blew his whistle again and sent them all back to practice. A few plays later, Buck practiced some of his honed skills on a freshman running back who was not amused by being body-slammed, or by losing the ball in the process. Buck helped him up and tried to give the guy a suggestion. "You need to hold the ball between both hands, and tuck it when you run, dude. Otherwise—"

"Hey," snarled the freshman. "You're not the quarterback anymore, that drill is over. So why don't you let me worry about running the ball?"

Dunheim blew his whistle to get their attention as he walked over to where the play ended. "Perfect hit, Buck. Runner, you need to protect yourself more on the flat."

Which was exactly what Buck had been telling him, but the kid wouldn't listen. Buck started to go back to the defensive huddle but the freshman was confused now, starting to fume, and he waved his arms and said, "But he—"

"But he what? Hit you too hard?" Dunheim laughed.

The freshman was upset. "I—"

"Just get back to the huddle."

The freshman kid wandered back. For the life of him, Buck couldn't remember the kid's name.

Buck knew the name of the next person he tackled, though: Billy Tibbs. Buck climbed off him quickly after the tackle, ready for the argument, but practice was ending and Billy spoke surprisingly, trying to encourage him. "Not bad, Buck, I think you rattled my back teeth."

Buck helped him up. "What?"

Billy shrugged. "You keep up these moves and this'll really be good. We'll knock those guys from Hopkins Central right into the middle of next week. . . ."

Buck watched Billy jog back over to the sidelines. Wild. Definitely a lot of changes to go through before anybody could get used to Tucker. He remembered then that he had to use the time Rachel got him to deal with researching his oral report, but there was more than that. Marshall was jogging over, and only then did Buck remember what the other thing was. As much as he hated to think about it, the cars awaited. . . .

TEN

They were working in the large two-car garage at Buck's house, having managed to coax Marshall's car into one final voyage across town. Buck's Uncle Vince was, of course, all for the phoenix idea. "Heck, I'm game for anything that'll get that junker off of my lawn." He lent them the garage space, tools, and access to other necessities they might need. Amanda's station wagon now sat in the driveway, out of the way, and Buck's junk Chevy sat alongside Marshall's in the garage.

Buck and Marshall stood waiting as Rachel started to survey the entire mess. Buck tried to stay interested, standing with his hands in his pockets, but he was really thinking about the oral report he was going to give the next day. He had a subject now, anyway: Prometheus, the Greek god who gave man fire. As for Marshall, he was getting a little overexcited about the whole thing, in Buck's opinion. "If this is the Mobile," said Marshall, "then what do we call Buck's car?"

"Well," commented Rachel as she examined them both, "since they don't make Impalas this big and useless anymore, why don't we think of it as Buck's Boat? Huh?"

"What?" Buck wasn't paying full attention to what was going on, but he shrugged. "It's not my car anymore," he said. "So whatever works is fine with me."

"This is going to be great," said Marshall, slapping his hands together. "We're going to create a phoenix. A beautiful new car rising from ashes of the old."

Rachel was wearing coveralls she'd borrowed from Vince. She'd brought an extra pair for both Buck and Marshall, but neither one of them was wearing theirs yet. She came out from looking deep under the Marsh Mobile's hood and shook her head. "It's not going to be a beautiful phoenix," she said. "It's going to be more like Frankenstein's monster."

Marshall took the cue immediately. He slumped over like Dr. Frankenstein's hunchback assistant and slurred, "Yes, master . . ."

"Hand me that lamp over there."

"Yes, master . . ." Marshall limped slowly and dramatically over to where the lamp lay. He plugged it in and brought it back to Rachel, who attached it to the open hood. Now they could see everything.

"Ugh . . . I don't like the looks of this engine block."

"You knew it was fizzed."

"I didn't know it was cracked."

"It's that bad?" asked Marshall.

"Not if you own a repair garage. Professional mechanics make a lot of money overhauling engines. For us, this means trouble. For starters we have to switch the engine block from Buck's Boat to your messed-up mobile."

Marshall nodded. "This won't take more than a couple of afternoons, will it?"

Rachel turned to Buck. "Is he crazy, or what?"

"No comment," said Buck. He started looking around the garage.

Marshall cleared his throat. "I sort of made this bet. . . ."

Rachel shook her head. "Don't tell me."

"The car has to be ready and fixed up by Friday."

"I told you not to tell me."

"Sorry."

"What kind of a crazy bet did you make?" Rachel had a wrench in her hand, and Marshall looked a little flushed, nervous.

"It was with Matt Kildare," he said

quickly. "I didn't have any choice. Matt was talking a lot of stupid talk, and I had to do something to shut him up."

Rachel nodded, taking a breath. "Okay. So what did you bet this Matt Kildare person?"

"Pizza."

Rachel took a minute, apparently thinking about it. "Okay," she said again. ":That's not too bad. You better go pay him."

"What?" Marshall looked like he was going to faint.

Rachel shrugged. "You better pay him the pizza you owe him."

"What? Buck!"

Buck cleared his throat and tried to come to Marshall's aid. "Uh . . . it wasn't exactly one pizza."

Rachel looked at Buck, and then back at Marshall. "Exactly how much pizza did you bet this Matt Kildare person?"

"Well, I've been figuring it out. At two men a pizza, plus three for Jim and Elwyn and three for Ray—"

"One guy is getting three pizzas?"

"Yeah," nodded Marshall. "Times that by the average cost . . . not including extra toppings, cheese, sausage, all that . . . we're looking at probably about seventy-five dollars' worth of pizza."

"What?" Rachel blinked.

Marshall swallowed. "Approximately. I

didn't have a calculator or anything to figure it all out with.''

"Arrrgh!" Rachel threw up her hands in frustration. She looked at Buck now as well. "You two football heads aren't exactly asking a lot, are you?"

Buck smiled at her. "Only your best, right Marsh? That's all we can ask."

Marshall nodded, but his smile was weaker. "Yeah. Your best, keeping in mind at all times that seventy-five dollars' worth of pizza means I don't eat lunch for the next eight years."

Rachel just shook her head again, and they went to work.

They broke off after nine P.M. with Rachel clicking off the dangling worklamp. All of them were covered in grime and sludge, and when Marshall's Mom arrived to pick him up he wandered off to the car holding his stomach, moaning about pizza and the high cost of living and the outrageous length of time modern auto repair took. Buck followed Rachel into the house and took a quick shower before doing some more research on his report. He was in the living room, rereading the article on Prometheus in the encyclopedia when Rachel stuck her head in the room. Nobody else was around and she said, "Hey, big brother."

Why did she keep calling him that? He hated to admit it, but he was starting to like it. She was the stranger and she was making him feel more at home than he'd ever felt before. He looked up and said, "Yeah?"

"You know we're never going to make it with the car by Friday, right?"

Buck shrugged. "Whatever."

"That's all? Whatever?"

"Sure. Whatever. It's not like we're trying to rescue astronauts trapped in space or anything. It's just a car."

"But I thought you cared about this. I thought you wanted to help Marshall."

Buck closed the encyclopedia. He couldn't stop thinking about how Rachel took that dive for him in class. *What are sisters for?* she'd asked, but Buck still felt funny about it. He looked at her and said, "You can't help everybody all the time, can you?"

Rachel frowned. "I don't know. A person's supposed to try, though. Right?"

Buck thought about it. "I guess."

Rachel nodded. "We'll do some more tomorrow. We'll see what happens then. Miracles happen, I suppose."

Which was true, miracles did happen. The next day's practice started out with a minor miracle: Matt Kildare got Buck and Marshall together and offered to call off the bet.

Buck could see that Marshall had to fight to keep the relief from sweeping across his face. "Uh, why?" he asked, trying to sound cool.

"Well," shrugged Matt. "I don't want to

take your money, Marsh. I know you can't afford it.''

"Thanks.''

"Besides, I heard that Rachel Tonachio girl was trying to help you guys, and I figured that any project involving you, Buck, and that superflake of a nutcase was something totally unfair to bet against.'' Matt laughed.

"Oh,'' Marshall nodded. Buck just listened. He was having thoughts of Chicago now, and he didn't know why.

Matt was still laughing. "That girl is great, though. Really. Like a house trying to fool burglars.''

"What do you mean?'' asked Buck then. He felt the muscles in his back tighten.

"I mean with that girl, all the lights are on but there's nobody home.''

"Oh,'' said Marshall again.

"How did you guys get mixed up with a loon like that in the first place?''

"The bet's on,'' said Buck.

"What?'' This was from Matt and Marshall, but the highest yelping voice was Marshall's. Buck's sudden announcement startled them both.

"You made a bet and now you're stuck with it, even if you are scared you're going to lose,'' said Buck. He stepped forward now, just inches from Matt's face. "And another thing . . .'' He jabbed a finger in Matt's chest, right between the numbers of his jersey. "Don't you ever, *ever* talk about my sister like that again."

Buck walked away then, and Marshall followed after him. Matt was still standing there stunned, and a lot of guys were talking back and forth. Buck noticed Billy Tibbs watching him as he left the locker room. *Whatever works,* he thought. The team was heading out for the practice field anyway.

After warm-ups, Coach Dunheim broke the team down into units and they ran a few plays at half-speed, mostly quick handoffs and sweeps with the wide receiver leading as a blocker because this was a play Doc thought they were weak in. Doc called these plays "ground gainers."

Billy Tibbs seemed to be getting irritated by the whole thing. His role in life was just taking the snap and handing the ball off. He wanted to engage in some pass patterns, some deviations, and obviously Doc intended to keep the game on the ground. On one play Buck and Ray deflected past John Bucek, who was leading as blocker, and they caught Matt Kildare in their famed pincer movement. He went down easily, but since it was a half-speed practice there was no heavy crunch and no reason for one. Matt got up, looking a little nervously at Buck, but managing a short laugh, saying, "I'm sure looking forward to some of that pizza tomorrow, eh, Buck?"

"Whatever works," said Buck.

The huddles ran pretty fast, with only seconds between plays and Billy Tibbs slapping his hands together. "Let's go!" Center Johnny Chappell took his firm grip on the ball and Billy lined up close behind, calling the signals: "Red Two! Red Two! Hut! Hut!"

The next play was another of Buck's fun wrestling matches with fullback Chip Moorehead. As always, Chip didn't go down easy and the half-speed of the run-through made things even more difficult for Buck since he was denied the old thunder-on-cleats power advantage. Still, he remembered some of the things Coach Dunheim had been passing along to him and he grappled for just a few seconds before he found an edge. Instantly Chip was toppling over with Buck on his back.

Chip bounced up immediately, impressed, laughing. "Not too shabby, you got me there. You saving any of that for the goons at Hopkins Central?" Chip gave him the power-fist salute and jogged back to the offensive huddle. On the sidelines a whistle was blowing. Doc's whistle. Practice was over.

Rachel was waiting outside of the locker room, and Buck shook his head, chuckling. "Why am I not surprised to see you here?"

"Because you're psychic?" asked Rachel. She nodded in answer to her own question. "You have the gift. I thought so from the first time I ever saw you. Come on, let's get going."

They were walking out of the gym building; their footsteps echoed in the empty hall. Buck looked at her. "Okay. Do you still want to be my sister?"

The question surprised Rachel. She was carrying her large straw purse and pulled it tight to her chest. "Yeah. I always wanted a brother. Do you care?"

Buck thought about it, then sighed. "Well, I never had a sister before. If I was to say yeah, you can be my sister, are there any special obligations that I should know about?"

"Yeah," she smiled. "You need to beat up people when I ask you to."

Buck shook his head, laughing. "You've got brothers confused with large attack dogs."

"Oh. Okay. Then you could just be around when I need you."

"Okay."

They hit the exit doors and started to walk toward home. The sun was fading, but the weather wasn't too bad. Rachel raised her head and said, "Even after I leave, I mean. Even after I'm not staying with your uncle anymore. You can't just stop because I go away for a few years. You still have to be my brother then."

Buck nodded. "Okay."

Rachel didn't say anything for a minute,

and they walked awhile. Buck told her about Matt offering to cancel the bet. "That's good," she said.

"I told him no."

"Say what?"

"I've got confidence in you."

"Okay," she said. "You did good on your report today in English, but I don't think that was the smartest bet you've ever made."

Buck shrugged. "Thanks for getting me the time to do the report. As for the rest, you know my line. Whatever—"

"Whatever works, yeah." They stopped to let a car go by on Terrence street, then crossed. Rachel shrugged. "Well, another zero in English doesn't bother me. I hate English anyway. This car thing could be rough."

"So how are the rest of your classes?"

Rachel shrugged again. "Doesn't matter. I don't know anybody there."

"I thought you were Miss Personality."

"Look who's talking, Mr. Football. A lot of the guys on your team think you're a homicidal maniac or something, and those are your so-called friends."

Buck frowned. "You let me worry about me, okay?"

"Sure, if you extend me the same courtesy."

She's got me there, Buck thought. He

swallowed. "Have you heard from your parents? Any news?"

"No. Things are going on, I guess. No news is good news, right?"

It was Buck's turn to shrug. "Right."

They started working on the car even before Marshall got there, which was probably just as well because they'd discovered that he tended to oversupervise and get in the way. For example, the left passenger door on the Boat was rusted through, right to the frame. "We'll need to replace this," said Rachel.

"Why?" asked Marshall. "Who cares about the door? Let's concentrate on the other things, get done, and go for a test drive."

"If we're going to do this at all, let's do it right," said Rachel.

"That's crazy, we don't have time for it. We need to concentrate on the important stuff."

"Look, who's doing most of the work here?" Rachel challenged.

Marshall looked her straight in the eye. "I thought it was a team effort."

Rachel snorted. "Some team."

"Okay, so let's take a vote." Marshall looked up. "Buck, you know what's at stake here, how important this is. What do you think? Do you think we should waste time with stupid things like doors, or what?"

Buck thought about it. He looked at Marshall, then he looked at Rachel and shrugged. "If we're going to do this at all, then let's go ahead and do it right."

"Yeah!" Rachel slammed her heavy wrench down on the rusted doorframe. A sudden hole appeared where the door handle had been. It took Buck and Marshall a couple of minutes to stop Rachel from giggling so they could press on.

They worked until nine o'clock again, and took up right after school the next day because Buck and Marshall didn't have to start getting ready for the Hopkins Central game until five o'clock. Once again they got a lot done before Marshall got there, and once again it was probably just as well because as soon as he arrived he managed to immediately drop a heavy boxed socket set on his foot. "Ouch," said Rachel in sympathy.

"Ouch and a half," grimaced Marshall. "That's my kicking foot."

"Are you all right?" asked Buck.

"Yeah, yeah, I'm just a terrified nervous wreck. I had a dream last night. Seventy-five dollars' worth of pizzas were dancing on my grave." He handed the socket set to Buck, who lifted the wrench from inside and asked exactly what it was he was supposed to do with it.

"We're going to change the points and plugs," said Rachel. She stuck her head deep under the hood. "Hand me the five-eighths," she said.

Buck sighed and started sifting through the metal box. Things were tense in the garage, but Rachel said, "We got a lot of the major things done, and we're a lot closer than we were before."

"Are we going to make it?" asked Marshall in an excited voice.

Rachel ignored him. "We're a lot closer than we were before."

Marshall appealed to Buck. "It's after four o'clock, and I'm going to fall apart at any minute. I'll be in no condition to play. How close are we?"

"I'm doing a tune-up right now," said Rachel from under the hood. "We should be able to drive to the game in the Boat."

"What?" Marshall ran over and stuck his head down to see. "You're kidding."

"Yes, I'm kidding."

"What?"

"Believe what you want. Just start getting ready to give this beast a jump." She crawled out from under the hood and pointed a finger. "Hook that electrode to the positive pole of that battery," she ordered.

"Electrodes?" said Marshall. He was all excited now and started hooking up the jumper cables. "This really is like Frankenstein."

Rachel wiped her hands on a rag and walked around the car to climb in. From inside the car she gave off an evil laugh.

Marshall looked over at Buck. "Where did you find that person?"

"I won her on a game show."

"Everybody stand back," ordered Rachel now that everything was set up.

Marshall jumped back beside Buck. Buck had to admit that he was a little nervous and excited himself. They were down to the wire now; win or lose they'd have to get down to the field pretty soon and start getting ready for the game. Marshall was a wreck. "Go ahead," Buck said to Rachel. "Go ahead and try it."

Rachel grinned. She gave Buck a thumbs-up and turned the key.

Nothing happened.

ELEVEN

Having had to practically drag him down to the school, Buck wasn't very surprised when Marshall refused to go into the locker room after Buck's Aunt Amanda dropped them off in the parking lot. "Are you crazy?" asked Marshall. "Matt Kildare is even now waiting for us in there, probably taking pizza orders from all the guys."

"Relax," sighed Buck. "How much can they eat?"

"How much can they eat? You said it yourself, in two words: Ray Burroughs. He didn't get that big nibbling on lettuce."

It was getting close to six-thirty, and Marshall finally gave up and went inside to start getting dressed. Buck followed him in and wondered if Marshall was maybe being a little stupid about the car not running, but then he thought, *why not? Why not be stupid about it?* Why were people always expected to brush off every disappointment in life as if it didn't mean anything at all?

Sheesh, thought Buck. He was starting to think like Rachel. Definitely a bad sign, especially considering that Rachel had been even more stubborn than Marshall. She was still crawling around under the car's hood when they had to leave for the game. Buck tried to ignore it all and stick to the matter at hand: beating Hopkins Central. Concentration was important, as Coach Dunheim emphasized and even Gordon Paluso had admitted. If you're not paying attention, you can easily get hurt.

Buck was getting dressed, and Marshall finally went to his locker and sat down on the bench beside a smug Matt Kildare. Matt was already half changed and he teased him. "I didn't hear any large automotive sounds coming from your direction in the parking lot, Marsh."

Marshall looked at Matt and took a breath. "I'll have you know it takes quite a while to wash and wax a car like that."

"I'll bet."

"Then you've got rust-proofing, and getting the little air freshener things installed."

"Remember," said Matt with that smug smile still on his face. "No anchovies, please."

Doc came out of the cage a few minutes later and said, "Heads up, I've got some points before we go out."

The guys settled down some and Doc started speaking. "Tonight we're going to emphasize ground gainers. I want to see a lot of power plays using Chip as the ball carrier, with Brad Palmer as leading blocker. I want to reemphasize: We're going to play a nice, safe game. No mistakes."

Doc waited for a reaction, and there was none. So he nodded and consulted his clipboard. "Some lineup adjustments here, so listen up. Danfield will be our primary kicker, and Pete Reisner was decent enough to show up on time tonight, so he'll be starting at wide receiver. Kildare, keep yourself sharp and play strictly defense for the first half at least. I want to see some interceptions out there tonight."

Just before the team took the field, Doc announced one final lineup change. "Grover, I hate to break up you and Brooks on the sidelines, but you need to start both ways tonight."

Buck felt all his muscles tighten. Here it came.

Doc looked at him. "Young, you sit out for a while. Okay, everybody, move! Everybody out on the field for warm-ups."

Buck didn't react right away. He sat there on the bench, unable to believe this was happening. What was going on? Why was he

being punished now after he'd worked so
hard in practice that week? He stood up and
walked over toward the head coach, trying
to think of something to say, a way to ask
what was happening. He swallowed and
opened his mouth. "Doc, I . . .''

"Buck, I've at least got to do this. You're
lucky you weren't cut. We'll talk about this
Monday, now go get out to the bench.''

Upset and humiliated, Buck bit his lower
lip in frustration. This wasn't fair, this was
absolutely not fair in any way, shape, or
form.

Buck's mind was spinning as the team
captains joined the referees at midfield.
Tucker won the toss, but Jeff Porter surprised the opposing captain by optioning to
kick off. This was on strict instructions from
Doc. There was a lot of strategy going into
tonight's game. Not that it mattered to
Buck. He settled down on the bench.

Marshall kicked off for Tucker, and for
once the luck went his way. He caught the
ball perfectly with the toe of his shoe, and
the crack of cleat against leather was heard
on both sides of the field. The Tucker fans
in the bleachers burst into cheers as the
Tucker defense rained down on the Hopkins
Central ball carrier. Ball *receiver* was a better term for it, since he didn't get to carry
it too far—he was smeared just after catching the ball on the thirty-yard line. The
crowd was really pumped up now as Central

broke their huddle and started to line up for the first offensive play of the night.

Buck watched the formation line up and the Central quarterback start to call his signals. The Central quarterback was Curtis Niswonger, who was tall and thin as a rail; Buck was interested in seeing how much real strength he'd display. As he'd seen in Chicago, some of the most unlikely-looking people were often powerhorses.

The crowd was waiting. Niswonger called a stutter count, and the ball was snapped. Buck read the play pretty close to correct, as Niswonger pitched out to one of his backs who immediately punched forward through the Tucker line for a gain of three yards. Buck was certain he could have nailed the guy short of the line of scrimmage, but he realized how smug and stuck-up that sounded. He also realized how easy it was to play sideline football and criticize everything you saw.

On the next play the ball was snapped and the quarterback, obviously sensing weakness there, threw himself forward with the center and guard leading as a wedge. They broke through the line for a gain of four yards before Norm Jackson brought the quarterback down. It wasn't a slap tackle, though. Norm had to hang onto the guy and drag him down; Niswonger was strong. Again, Buck was pleased with himself for reading the guy properly. He'd remember that for later, if a later came.

What was it Doc said to him? We'll talk about it on Monday? Buck couldn't help feeling a chill at the thought. Forget about just not starting; did that mean he wasn't going to get to play at all? Were they taking action on the principal's suggestion after all?

Tucker stopped the Central drive without allowing a single first down, forcing them to punt. Tucker's Al Lucente snagged the ball deep in his own territory, and was snagged himself at the twenty-nine after a fifteen-yard sprint. Not a great return, but not a bad one, either. Buck looked at the scoreboard: seven minutes left in the first quarter.

Coach Dunheim wandered away from his position beside Doc and down to the bench. Buck tried not to seem like he was resentful about being benched. He didn't want to be a little kid about it, ready to take his football and go home. Dunheim smacked his clipboard with his flat, open palm. His eyes were shining and he asked, "So how do you think we're doing?"

Buck swallowed and said, "Their quarterback likes to run."

Dunheim nodded. "So does Doc."

"Maybe they should get together."

Dunheim laughed, then he said, "Listen, Buck, I know you hate not starting, but let's see what Doc does for the second half."

Buck looked up. "I'm fine. You know what I say, right? Whatever works."

"Whatever works. Right." Dunheim wandered back up the sidelines.

The first quarter wound down, and Tucker's offensive drive carried over into the second, but was also unsuccessful. Central surprised them in the second quarter, though, by scoring back-to-back touchdowns. Both scores were based on power runs and screen passes and the agility of their backfield. It wasn't that the Tucker defense was folding, only that they were caught looking the wrong way a couple of times and got burned.

Tucker's offense had yet to get going, although Chip and Brad managed some good runs together and gained several first downs. Marshall also managed to put Tucker on the scoreboard with a thirty-six-yard field goal. The score was 14–3 when the half ended with the gun.

The team retired to the locker room for the old Knute Rockne speech they expected. The Tucker High School marching band took the field behind them, breaking into a variation of the music from the *Rocky* movies. Buck was embarrassed going in, because he was like every other second- or third-stringer: He hadn't even worked up a sweat. Billy Tibbs took off his helmet and accepted a cup of Gatorade from one of the managers. Perspiration was rolling down his face and he swallowed the drink greedily, then he made his way over to Doc, who was now standing in front of the cage.

Billy started to question Doc, and it didn't take long before everyone could hear their heated argument. Billy wanted to take the game to the air, but Doc was committed to the ground, convinced of the unseen power of the Hopkins Central defense. Billy pressed the point. "How do we know they can stop the pass? Their quarterback runs, and they can stop a run. I wonder if they can really play a good pass defense. I wonder if—"

Doc cut Billy off. "There's only three things that can happen when you pass, Billy, and two of them are bad: interceptions and incompletes."

"But think of all the ground we can gain."

"Think of everything we've got to lose."

"We're down fourteen to three."

"Yes, and we've got the entire second half to go yet."

Billy took a deep breath and waited. Doc said, "Keep the game on the ground, and that clock will wind down. If we keep the ball away from them while we're killing the clock, they can't score. And if they can't score, they can't win. All we need to win is two touchdowns."

Which made sense to Buck, but he had a hard time keeping his mind on the technicalities of the game. All Buck wanted was a chance to play. A chance he was by now sure wasn't coming.

Billy crumpled up his paper cup and tossed it away. "One thing's for sure," he said. "If I'm going to do anything in there I need the ball, which means a more aggressive defense. And I need time in the pocket, which means an offensive line without any holes in it." Billy took another breath and said, "I need Buck Young out there with me."

Buck blinked. What? He looked over and saw Billy winking at him. Buck's heart felt like it might rip right through his chest.

Doc hesitated a minute, then dismissed his hesitation. "Buck!"

Buck was beside Doc in a heartbeart. "Sir."

"When the offense goes out again, you go in for Grover on offense. I'm going to make some more changes, give some guys a rest. Why don't you play both ways for a while."

"Yes, sir."

Billy slapped Buck on the back. "Let's win this one."

"You got it, kid."

The first few plays of the half were going to be crucial. They would set the momentum for the rest of the game. The score was Central 14, Tucker 3, and Tucker was going to receive the kickoff, thanks to Doc's insistence at the coin toss that receiving be deferred.

The Central kicker, number sixty-three, kicked the ball high, and Billy had to wait under it for a while. This gave the defenders plenty of time to move downfield, and even with a lot of heavy blocking Billy wound up getting splattered pretty good on Tucker's own thirty-five-yard line. The first play Billy called was a quick end around, with John Bucek coming off the left end to take the ball around the right, with Buck and Matt Kildare leading as blockers. They made pretty good ground with that, attaining another first down and improving their field position, except somebody stepped on Buck's left hand and ripped it up with a cleat. It hurt like crazy, but after missing the entire first half there was no way Buck was going to take himself out for a minor injury, even if it was bleeding a little. He got back to the huddle as quickly as he could.

"Great, great," said Billy as they huddled up again. Bucek was breathing pretty hard and he just nodded. "Let's try the ripper, on two." Billy said.

John Bucek smiled, and it was a very devious smile. "Doc won't like it."

Billy took a breath. "Doc's not out here. The ripper on two. Ready . . . Break!"

The huddle slapped all of their hands together in fierce unison, then broke to form up at the line of scrimmage.

"Down!"

As a unit, all the guys on the line hunched over.

"Ready!"

The line came back up again. Billy yelled, "Set!" and the line dropped back into their three-point stance. Buck remembered to growl, but the guy across from him didn't seem too shaken up by it.

"Hut! *Hut*!"

Buck exploded forward, using his legs like pistons to throw all of his weight into the defensive guard in one shocking motion. All around him he could hear grunting and slamming and the heavy footsteps of the runners. Some defense guys started screaming warnings. "Pass! Pass!" Only they might have been too late. Billy rocketed the ball away seconds before being trampled by intruding defenders. Matt Kildare caught the pass for a twelve-yard gain and another first down.

The momentum had shifted, and there was a lot of excitement in the huddle now. Guys were slapping their hands together and talking. "Hold it down!" said Billy. He hesitated only a second. "Let's sneak one up the middle. Buck will be my point man; Ray, make us a hole. On one. Ready . . . Break!"

Buck grunted as he set himself up at the line of scrimmage. The pain in his hand didn't seem anywhere near as bad now. "Hut!" screamed Billy, and Buck slammed forward, leading Billy through a pocket.

Buck got smashed, but Billy managed to make a substantial gain. On the next play Brad Palmer led Chip Moorehead right up the middle for the score. Central 14, Tucker 9. Marshall kicked the extra point, to make the score 14-10.

The score remained that way for the rest of the third quarter, as the two teams settled into a grueling pattern—each would advance to about midfield before the opposing defense stopped the drive and forced a punt. And as the game wound down through the fourth quarter, with the two squads trading possessions, it looked as if only a mistake by one of them would make the difference.

With less than a minute to play, the mistake came. Central was trying to run out the clock by keeping the ball on the ground and in the hands of its surest ballcarriers. One of the Central fullbacks was just about to turn upfield on an end run when free safety John Bucek, anticipating the move, took a chance and tackled the guy high, around the middle, trying to strip the ball. It worked. The ball sprang loose and in the mad scramble Bucek himself came up with the ball. Tucker had possession on the Central forty-two-yard line with fifteen seconds left to play—enough time for two plays.

It seemed to Buck as if his fellow Tigers could hardly drag themselves back to the huddle. He slapped backs, exhorting them on. The guys gathered in a tight circle so they could hear Billy over the crowd noise. Tibbs called two quick plays and said, "This is for the money. Ready . . . Break!"

The first was a short pass, complete to John Bucek, but Bucek failed to get out of bounds, which would have stopped the clock. The Tigers raced back to the line to set up for the next play—their last. The crowd tensed up, waiting; everyone seemed to be holding their breath.

Billy called his signals, making an audible change to the play. "Red Six!" he shouted to his right. "Red Six!" he screamed to his left. Buck knuckled down and almost grinned. Billy had just called the same desperation pass that Buck had used on his last play as quarterback, at the scrimmage . . . when? A couple of weeks before, maybe? It seemed like years had passed since then.

"Hut! *Hut!*"

Buck exploded forward, buying Billy time with his body, but being careful not to risk a holding penalty. Any penalty against the offense would end the game.

The crowd went crazy. Billy shot the ball off like a rocket and everybody could see it was a perfect pass. This was it! This was it! Pete Reisner snared the ball on the sideline, and took off, hotly pursued, just a few feet ahead of the defenders. Buck found himself screaming like the rest. "Go! Go!"

Reisner had a lead of only inches now, as two defenders reached out and grappled for

him. But it was too late. He crossed into the
end zone just as they nailed him, both defenders crashing down on Pete's back too
late.

"Yeah!" Buck screamed. "Yeah!" Ray
Burroughs was there and he slapped Buck
on the back in congratulations and turned
to Norm Jackson. "Yeah!"

Only Norm wasn't smiling, and there were
whistles blowing.

What happened?

No. Buck felt his stomach do a roll as he
saw what had happened. No. Only it was
true: The referees were calling the ball out
of bounds at the point of reception. Pete
charged back down the field, obviously enraged, but Coach Dunheim stepped out to
grab him. The Central players were now going crazy in their own right now. Time was
gone and they'd beaten Tucker in a
squeaker.

As the players left the field, Buck felt a
few slaps on the back and muttered, "Good
game." Somebody in the parking lot was
blowing on his car horn in celebration—
obviously a Central fan who'd driven over—
and Buck and the guys ignored them. "Great
game, Buck!" some of the guys said to him.
"That's the way to play ball."

John Bucek fell into step beside Buck. He
nodded toward the parking lot, where Marshall and some guys were making a fuss.

"You'd think we won the game or something."

And why not? thought Buck. He saw Amy Lowell from the theater standing with some of her friends over by the edge of the field, and he resolved to talk to her before the end of the night, or die in the attempt. And he decided to tease Bucek. "Well, John, you know what Mekler of Chicago said. Every day is a victory."

Honk! Honk! *Honk*!

Trying not to be irritated, Buck twisted around to see who was having the close relationship with the car horn and got the shock of his life: It was Rachel, honking and gunning the engine of the now obviously functioning Phoenix Mobile. Marshall and some of the other guys from the team were already down there with her, making Rachel the heroine of the hour. Somehow she had managed the miracle, and she had gotten the stupid thing running and drove it over, just to save Marshall's silly bet. Crazy. Rachel didn't even have a driver's license.

Everybody took a break to shower and change, and then hurried back out to the parking lot to admire the Phoenix Mobile, grabbing cups of soda to drink on the way. Amy was there, and Buck offered her a soda.

"Thanks," said Amy. She smiled at him. Amy was as impressed with the car as anyone, but just when Buck was going to ask her to come along on the pizza trip, Rachel came over to him, grinning. "*Excuse* me," she said, with mock irritation in her voice.

Buck swallowed, a little nervous. Amy looked at him and Rachel expectantly; her smile seemed a little weaker.

"Aren't you going to introduce us?" asked Rachel.

"Uh . . . Amy . . ."

"Hi, Amy. I'm Buck's little sister. How you doing?"

Amy smiled again, and this time it was wide and beaming.

John Bucek saw Rachel and came over to the group. It was obvious Bucek liked Rachel. "Want to come with us for pizza?" he asked. "Matt's buying, the victim of his own foolish ego, and I'm in the position to guarantee extra cheese."

"Sure," said Rachel. Buck asked Amy at the same time, and she also agreed. Terrific! Rachel shifted her weight from her right foot to her left then, and punched Buck in the shoulder, saying, "Hey, I just found out I'm going home tomorrow. Back to Boston. I guess Mom has a few things straightened out."

Amy looked a little confused, but Buck said, "Great, that's really great."

Matt was wandering around the car, amazed and embarrassed to admit it, but finally he said, "Hey, I can't afford to buy pizza for everyone. Give me a break."

"You made a bet," said Ray, rising up to his full pizza-eating size.

"Yeah, but—"

Bucek left Rachel's side for a minute to put his arm around Matt and said, "Maybe we can make a deal here, Matthew. . . ."

Matt looked suspicious. "What kind of deal?"

"Well . . . since you asked. As you know, some funding cuts have put the Chess Club in danger of folding, since they've been unable to attract the fifteen members they need to match mandatory attendance."

Matt groaned. "What does that mean in English, John?"

"It means if you will join the Chess Club, I'll help pay for the pizza."

"The Chess Club? Are you crazy!"

"It's only one activity hour a week. You'll love the game. Really."

There was more groaning, but Matt surrendered. "All right, I'm nailed."

"Football players on the Chess Club," muttered Ray Burroughs. "What will happen to us next?"

Rachel smiled. She made an announcement to everyone. "I know what's going to happen next. I think you guys are going to be champions."

At first nobody said anything, and Buck felt a little uncomfortable. After all, the game had not exactly been the stuff of champions. There was potential, but it still needed to be worked at. He said "I don't know about that."

Rachel nodded again. "Well, I think so, anyway."

"Champions?" bellowed Marshall, now standing on the hood of the car. "We're going a lot further than being just champions. They may have to rename the school after us."

John Bucek interrupted. "The school is already called Tucker, Marsh."

Marshall shook his head. "Forget Tucker, I'm talking about the Tigers."

"Tiger High School?" asked Jim.

"You wait and see. Rachel is right; at least she has confidence. Not to reflect, but this is like my report on the phoenix bird in English, and my . . . I mean *our* triumph, with the birth of the Phoenix Mobile. Tonight's game, that was just the ashes, and from these ashes the Tigers are going to rise and give everybody the bird!"

"Airborne assault!" called Ray Burroughs. Buck pulled Amy quickly out of the way and a dozen crushed soda cups took flight and bounced off Marshall before he finally ducked away, jumping off the car and escaping.

So far this season, the Tucker Tigers have been winning half their games! They owe much of their good fortune to fullback, Chip Moorehead's fantastic offensive plays. But, all the cheering and praise has gone to Chip's head and unless he keeps his cool, he just might ruin the team effort needed to take the Tigers to the top. Don't miss:

BLITZ #3
GUTS AND GLORY